THE MAN IN THE MIDDLE

Caine emerged onto the road and headed south. He hadn't slept for sixteen hours, yet he didn't feel tired. Nervous tension from the meeting with his brother, he figured—plus an intuitive sense of danger. He traveled a mile and entered a region of low but rugged hills dotted with wild shrubs. When he came out on the other side, three men, all mounted and in a line, faced him. He stopped. six eyes bore into him in studied silence.

"Howdy, Simon Caine," said the one in the middle.

Caine shifted his shoulders, but otherwise didn't react at all.

"I said howdy."

"I'm afraid you've mistook me for somebody else," Caine said.

"Not only a sniping pistolero, but a liar, too. You're coming with us, Caine. It don't matter to me whether it's your rump or your belly in the saddle."

"Let me pass," Caine said.

"No," said the man in the middle as he drew his pistol.

CAINE'S TRAIL

Cameron Judd

BANTAM BOOKS
NEW YORK • TORONTO • LONDON • SYDNEY • AUCKLAND

CAINE'S TRAIL
A Bantam Book/ September 1989

ISBN 0-553-28244-1

Published simultaneously in the United States and Canada

Bantam Books are published by Bantam Books, a division of
Bantam Doubleday Dell Publishing Group, Inc. Its trademark,
consisting of the words "Bantam Books" and the portrayal of a
rooster, is Registered in U.S. Patent and Trademark Office and
in other countries. Marca Registrada. Bantam Books, 666 Fifth
Avenue, New York, New York 10103.

PRINTED IN THE UNITED STATES OF AMERICA

O   0 9 8 7 6 5 4 3 2 1

CAINE'S TRAIL

Chapter 1

His name was Rubio. Clad in white, loose clothing and a broad-brimmed hat that clung to his head despite the wind, he ran through the bright Texas moonlight, and in his fist he held a coin.

A hound bayed at the boy; in a nearby pen chickens fluttered and clucked, disturbed by his passing. In the shadows beneath a porch a prowling cat lifted its slitted eyes and watched him dart by.

Beside the gently cambered road ahead stood the imposing, solemn house where Garth Kensington slept alone on his big bed, dreaming whatever are the dreams of an old and dying man. In the moonshadow of his mansion stood a much smaller frame house. Rubio ran to the door of that smaller house, paused to catch his breath, and rapped.

Inside, Brice James bolted upright in his bed. Knocking sounded again through the dark house. Brice rose and put on his trousers, slipping galluses over his bare shoulders. He walked down the hallway, looking into the room where his son was just beginning to awaken.

Rubio was about to knock again when Brice opened the door. "Rubio?" Brice said. "What is it?"

"Señor James, there is a man waiting for you at the old tower. He sent me here to tell you to come."

"A man?"

"Sí. A tall man. He did not say his name. He is alone."

Brice frowned, intrigued but a little concerned. "The tower," he repeated. "Thank you, Rubio."

1

The boy flashed a smile brighter than the moon. "He paid me this," he said, holding up his coin, then turned and ran back into the night.

Brice closed the door. His son stood in the hallway.

"Don't go, Pa."

Brice scratched the back of his neck. "It might be important, Keelan. Don't worry, I'll be back safe and sound. You go on back to bed."

The night was chilly, in marked contrast to the sweltering heat of the day. Brice thrust his hands into his jacket pockets as he trudged down the road. He walked with the slight limp that was his ever present reminder of his part in the failed fight for the Confederacy.

The farther Brice walked, the more uncomfortable he became. He thought of turning back but already saw the dark tower ahead, a stone spire thrusting toward the blue-black sky. The tower was all that remained of a chapel that had been part of an old rancho here. Brice trailed his gaze up its length, seeing the black outline of the old bell in the open belfry at the top—and then a shadow moved across the bell's dark face.

Someone was in the bell tower, watching him.

Brice edgily strode forward. He could not see the figure in the belfry anymore; perhaps he had not seen it at all. The night and the stark old tower could stir numinous imaginings in a man.

It was dark in the base of the tower, and deathly silent. Vermin scurried nearby. The moon sailed high above and cast its light through the open door behind Brice.

Brice found a candle in a holder on the wall and lit it. Light spilled onto the stair that spiraled up inside the tower.

"Hello?" he said. No answer came.

Swallowing his fear, he began climbing. Hot wax dripped on his fingers and solidified.

"Hello?"

Still no answer. He continued up, limping more badly now. Through a tiny window in the tower wall he saw the moonlit expanse of naked Texas landscape. The sight made him feel enclosed. "Is anybody here?"

Near the top he stopped. The candle's feeble glow lit the shape of a tall man standing at the top of the stairs. He was lean, stood with one leg cocked slightly to the side, and appeared to be looking back down at Brice, though Brice could not see his face. The iron bell swung gently in the wind behind the man.

The man's voice was soft but deep. "Hello, brother."

Brice dropped the candle; it snuffed out. "Simon!" he exclaimed.

"So you were in the Bitterroots all those years," Brice said. "I never knew if you were alive or dead."

"Occasionally there seemed little difference between the two," Simon Caine said wryly. He was leaning against one of the four stone pillars at the corners of the open belfry, paradoxically looking relaxed but also as tense as a wound clock spring.

"Still your grim view of the world," Brice said. "I recall when people saw you as lighthearted, and me as melancholy."

"We've lived different lives. Makes us different men," Simon Caine said. He reached into his pocket and came out with a small cigar. He dug for a match, then seemingly changed his mind. From his perch he scanned the mesquite flats below. Brice noted it and knew Simon Caine was looking for pursuers. Simon had declined to smoke because the flare of the match might expose him.

"Government still after you, Simon?"

Simon Caine nodded.

"How have you lived?"

"Off the land, mostly. I took a sort of job sometime back, guiding some folks through the mountains. But that didn't work out like it was supposed to. I got to see Jake Armitage again, though. You remember Jake?"

Brice nodded. "How is he?"

"He's dead. Got himself knifed by a young buck."

"Oh."

"You don't seem too sorry."

"It's not that. I just think Jake tended to steer you wrong sometimes."

"You sound as much like a preacher as ever."

"I'm not. I gave it up—just didn't feel right for me, somehow, after I preached Marcus and Nancy's funeral."

Mention of his wife and son's funeral sent an expression of sadness across Caine's angular features. He shifted the subject. "I heard you work for Garth Kensington now. A mighty rich man."

"Not anymore. He's stone-cold broke. There's few who know it yet, but the Kensington empire is about to fall. First Agatha dies, and now this."

"Losing a wife is a hard thing."

"You know she was Garth Kensington's daughter? That's right—I married into the family. She was pretty, sweet as she could be. Bore me a fine son. It was consumption that took her."

"Mighty sorry, James . . . Brice, I mean. Can't get used to calling you that."

A silent moment passed. Brice asked, "Why did you come here, Simon?"

"A man ought to see his little brother every now and then."

"Even a brother who changes his name to hide his kinship to you?"

Brice watched for Simon's reaction, but if the words stung, Caine didn't show it. "Does your boy know about me?" Caine asked.

Brice shook his head. "I never even told Agatha. She wouldn't have known how to take being the kin of an outlaw."

"And how do you take it? Have you forgiven me yet for—what did you call it?—shaming the family name?"

"It isn't me who has a problem forgiving, Simon. It's you."

"Could you have forgiven the murder of your wife and child? Could you watch a man butcher your kin and then just walk away from it?"

"But you became a butcher yourself. You murdered for murder."

"It was payback. Justice."

"No," Brice said. "It was bushwhacking. Lynching. Riding with the likes of Bloody Bill and Quantrill. That's not justice by any stretch."

The wind made the rusted iron bell hum. "Maybe I shouldn't have come back," Simon said. "I just took a hankering to see you again."

Brice spoke more softly now. "Where are you heading?"

"First to see Drew Strahan. He's hermiting out between Van Horn and the Rio Bravo. After that, Mexico. Got some business there."

Simon Caine swept his brother with a head-to-toe glance, as if trying to impress his image into his mind. "Maybe I'll see you again."

Caine went to the stairs.

"Don't come back again, Simon," Brice said.

Caine stopped for a half-second but didn't turn. He descended the stairs. Brice remained in the tower a few minutes, fighting an inner struggle. Suddenly he bolted down the stairs as best his bad leg would let him.

"Simon!"

He ran out of the dark tower into the moonlight.

"Simon!"

But there was no one there.

"A drunk?" Keelan said quizzically. "Why would a drunk send for you in the middle of the night, Pa?"

"It's somebody I knew back in the war," Brice said, sitting on the side of the bed and pulling off his boots. He was glad to have an excuse not to look into his son's face while he lied. "Bill Rawlins is his name. He wanted money. I gave him what I had in my pocket and he left. Now you go back to bed."

For Brice, rest was fitful and fleeting. An hour after he lay down he still was awake and restless.

Why had Simon come back after all this time, bringing old memories and feelings that disturbed him?

Maybe it was because Simon Caine and bad times like these always seemed cojoined in the life of Brice James, known in his earlier days as James Brice Caine.

Brice rolled over, brooding. A few minutes later he at last fell asleep.

Years in the Bitterroot Mountains had sharpened Simon Caine's senses. He felt the rider long before he heard him, and he heard him long before he saw him. Caine veered his Appaloosa into the roadside rocks. There he waited.

Down the moonlit road the rider came. Broad, long-haired, he was fat and heavy in the saddle; his bay's back sagged like the middle of a worn-out bed tick.

Another greasy gunman. Maybe a border bandit or a bounty hunter. Caine sat silent in the darkness. The rider passed. Then Caine's Appaloosa snorted.

The rider halted, peering into the rocks. His hand moved toward his pistol.

Caine felt a familiar tensing of his shoulders and quickening of his pulse. He felt the Navy Colt in its holster the way he could feel his feet in his boots.

But the fat rider turned away, touching rowels to flanks, and started down the road again. Caine held his breath until he was gone, then slumped for a moment, letting tension drain from him.

He could have taken the man easily, but he was glad he had not had to. He was weary of killing and of running—the two things that had dominated his life since the long-ago day a drunken Union officer named Robert Montrose had murdered his family back in the Calfkiller Valley in Tennessee.

Caine emerged onto the road again and headed south. He hadn't slept for sixteen hours, yet he didn't feel tired. Nervous tension from the meeting with Brice, he figured—plus an intuitive sense of danger.

Caine chewed a cigar, unwilling to light it. He was looking forward to morning, when he could pull into some shady recess and sleep.

He traveled a mile and entered a region of low but rugged hills dotted with wild shrubs. When he emerged onto the road on the other side, three men, all mounted and in a line, faced him. He stopped. Six eyes bored into him in studied silence.

"Howdy, Simon Caine," said the one in the middle.

Caine shifted his shoulders but otherwise did not react at all.

"I said howdy."

"I'm afraid you've mistook me for somebody else," Caine said. "My name's Robert Cole."

"Not only a sniping *pistolero*, but a liar, too," the man said. "You're coming with us, Caine. It don't matter to me whether it's your rump or your belly in the saddle."

"Let me pass," Caine said.

"No," said the man in the middle as he drew his pistol.

Chapter 2

Keelan James ate silently, watching his grandfather from the corner of his eye. Garth Kensington, humped over in his wheelchair, was talking to a whispering, gesturing employee, and whatever the employee was saying apparently displeased the old man. Kensington's heavy brows writhed over his gray eyes like twin caterpillars.

At last Kensington impatiently waved the employee out with his thin white hand.

The dining room door opened and Brice entered, baggy eyes evidencing his lack of sleep. He dropped heavily into a chair beside Keelan. A black woman built like a walking cookstove bustled in with a steaming china pot and poured Brice a cup of coffee, for which he muttered thanks.

Kensington's voice was an almost falsetto squeak as he said, "Brice, there were three men killed last night not two miles from here. Dead on the road, shot through the head. Hoofmarks showed there was only one other man there, so it must have been him that killed them. Three men gunned down by one."

Brice closed his eyes. *Simon, you carry death wherever you go.*

Kensington muttered something about dangerous times and trouble a-brewing and how it probably had something to do with that sorry desert bandit Cato Blake, all the while with knife and fork tremblingly slicing his four fried eggs into a yellow-white hash. Keelan looked away, hating to see his grandfather in his dotage. The boy sensed the old man must die soon, and that scared him. Losing his mother had ingrained in him a hatred of death.

The maid brought in Brice's plate. She set it before him and exited, but he pushed it away as the kitchen door wheezed shut behind her.

"It's getting so a man can't feel safe in his own home," Kensington muttered in his tremulous voice. He looked at Brice. "You look puny."

"Didn't sleep well," Brice said irritably.

"Drink some coffee, then. You got a pile of ledgers to go over."

"I'll drink coffee if I want it," Brice snapped. He rose and stalked out of the room. Keelan watched him, his eyes big, then turned to his grandfather, wondering how the old man would react to Brice's outburst.

But Kensington had not even noticed it. He was eating, smacking his lips loudly as little dribbles of egg leaked onto his chin.

Outside, Brice stood on the lower porch of the big house, taking in without enjoyment a magnificent view of this section of West Texas that had come to be known as Kensington, after the ranch of which this house was the headquarters. The house itself, when viewed from out on the plains, was no less than splendid. Its three stories rose from the barren landscape like a mirage. With its gingerbreaded columns and two-level balcony porches, the edifice suggested a steamboat sailing across the land on shimmering waves of rising heat.

Brice missed Agatha badly at this moment. Life was so miserably uncertain right now: the Kensington financial empire in ruin, and Garth himself ready to die, leaving Brice to deal with the hopeless finances of the estate. And now to top it off, Simon had come back again, unwelcome and disturbing as ever.

Brice chuckled mirthlessly. Fate and circumstances were imps too cruelly mischievous for him to understand. He turned and limped back into the house, feeling terribly depressed.

*　　*　　*

With great effort Garth Kensington rolled his squeaking wheelchair through his house. Often he had to stop and cough, and every spasm wrenched and hurt.

One of his servants, a handsome and powerfully built black man of about twenty, approached. "Let me help you, Mr. Kensington." The young man took the grips of the chair. "Where to, sir?"

"The office, Orion."

Orion pushed the chair along. Kensington leaned back, resting from his prior exertion. Though he would never thank Orion, Kensington was grateful for his help. Orion was the son of Tandy Jones, who had once been Kensington's slave but now was his servant—a special one, for his long association with Kensington had carved him a notch in the family structure itself. Tandy's late wife had raised Kensington's daughter Agatha after Agatha's mother had died from consumption. When that same disease had finally claimed Agatha herself, Tandy had felt the loss almost as much as Garth and Brice. He sang a dirge over her grave when they buried her.

Orion and Garth reached the batwings that hung in the doorway of the old parlor that housed Kensington's messy office. Orion pushed the wheelchair through, and the batwings flapped closed behind him, shuddering on their hinges.

"Anything else, Mr. Kensington?"

"No, Orion. This is fine."

"Just call if you need me." Orion turned and left.

Brice was seated at a small corner table with ledgers and papers before him. His expression was somber. Kensington saw it and wilted a little farther down into his chair.

"Bad?"

"It's worse every time I go over it," Brice said.

Kensington was quiet for a moment. "Then go over it again," he said. "There's got to be something we can do."

"But I've looked at it ten dozen times already."

"Make it ten dozen and one," Kensington snapped. He coughed painfully, wheeled his chair around, and left.

Brice felt deflated and tense. He rose and went to the window. It seemed ridiculous to dig further into Kensington's records of ruin. At one time a brilliant financier who had made a fortune in cattle, horses, and mining, Kensington had in the past five years boxed himself into a monetary prison with chancy investments Brice and others had warned him against. Any number-wrangler in the nation could investigate Kensington's books and the conclusion would be the same: bankruptcy.

A small figure darted across the yard toward the house. Brice smiled and opened the window. He leaned out, his hands on the sill.

"Hello, Keelan," he said.

The boy grinned. His exuberance was to Brice a welcome contrast to the darkness of this closed room and the oppressive futility of this work.

"Tandy's taking me for another ride on the buckboard," Keelan said. "Way out on the back road. You want to come, Pa?"

"I wish I could," Brice said, and he meant it. "Your grandfather wants me to go over his books again."

"Oh," Keelan said. Books and business were alien to him, unrealities belonging to a grown-up world. "We're going right up along the creek, too."

Brice smiled. In Keelan's bright face he saw the only remaining incarnation of his late wife, and that both pleased and saddened him. "Have a good time," Brice said.

"I will, Pa."

Keelan ran lightly across the yard toward the adobe carriage house where Tandy and the buckboard awaited. Brice faltered for a moment, almost yelling after Keelan to wait, he would come along after all. But from somewhere in the dark belly of the house he heard Garth Kensington's rattling cough and was reminded again of his duty.

Sadly he turned away from the window as Tandy and Keelan clattered off in a cloud of dust down the road that led to a tree-lined creek a mile to the south.

J. W. Fadden, a man seemingly made of wire and whiskers, sat astride his old gelding and rolled a cigarette. Before him stretched rolling dun-colored land, its vegetation of waist-high mesquite spaced like hairs on the head of a balding man. Fadden was staring at Kensington's mansion, an architectural majesty encircled by barns and stables like a king surrounded by attendants. Even from this far away, Fadden could smell the money this place represented—and it was a smell he liked.

Two men, also mounted, were with him. One of them, a thin Mexican, pointed and said, "Look. He's coming."

A rider was approaching; he was a dark speck growing larger with a dust cloud trailing behind. Fadden and his partners watched and waited until the rider reached them.

The rider sagged like an overstuffed feed bag over both sides of his saddle. He had been blond once; now his hair was colorless. A ragged mustache blanketed his upper lip and hung over his mouth so that when he raised his dirty bandana to wipe dust from his lips, he had to lift the mustache out of the way.

"They're hooking up the buckboard right now," the newcomer said. "Just the boy and Tandy the old nigger. You cut south a mile, fast as you can go, and you can catch 'em right at the creek."

"Mighty fine, Mr. Scruggs." Fadden produced an envelope and handed it to the man. "Count it if you want. It's all there."

Hosea Scruggs smiled. His breath wheezed deep in his chest. "I trust you."

He put the envelope beneath his shirt and touched his hat. He spurred his horse with his small Mexican spurs and galloped back toward the Kensington ranch.

The Mexican lifted a scope-mounted sniper's rifle from its saddle holster. "Let it be, Juan," Fadden said. "The shot might draw attention."

"But Seahorn said—"

"Seahorn ain't here. We'll do it my way. Come on, gentlemen. Let's head for that creek."

The buckboard clattered along the back road. Tandy's untrained baritone rang out an old drinking song, making Keelan laugh because he knew he wasn't supposed to hear songs like that. But Tandy seldom followed the rules—one of the things that made Keelan love him so.

Tandy also drove the buckboard too fast, which impressed Keelan even more. The fast rides always seemed daring and exhilarating to the boy, and today's was even better than usual.

They made a turn and passed a crossroads, then came to a rainwater-filled waterhole surrounded by grasses and mesquite. The hole was fed by a tiny creek a man could step across without a strain, but it provided good water for livestock except in the driest times. They heard the creek ahead, splashing along through a brake of cottonwoods that towered above the scrub brush.

They entered the cool, shaded brake. The buckboard clattered along, but suddenly Tandy reined back on the horses.

A downed tree blocked the road just ahead. It was an old deadfall that had lain in the brake beside the road for months. But now it lay across the road itself.

"How did that get there, Tandy?" Keelan asked.

The old black man shook his head. He reached to the buckboard floor and picked up the shotgun, then descended from his seat.

"Why are you getting that, Tandy?"

"You just stay put and keep quiet, Keelan."

Three riders emerged from the brake, leading one saddled-but-riderless horse. They positioned themselves on the road near the deadfallen cottonwood. All three looked like dusty saddlebums with dirt-stained, whiskered faces. One stayed slightly ahead of the other two; he was as filthy as his companions but had an air that marked him as their leader.

J. W. Fadden nodded at Tandy and said, "Howdy there, Toby. Got you a problem?"

"My name ain't Toby."

Fadden smiled. "Your kind's all Toby to me, and you'd best remember how to call a man sir," he said. Then Fadden looked at Keelan, almost hungrily. He touched his hat. "Hello, boy."

Keelan stared back unresponsively. Tandy remained firmly planted, the shotgun nearly horizontal before him, ready to be swung up and fired.

Tandy said to Keelan, "We'll be heading back."

"No, Toby, you won't," Fadden said. "Not until I'm ready for you to."

Keelan spoke up bravely: "You're on my grandpa's land, and he wouldn't want you talking that way to Tandy."

"Really? He likes the nigger, huh? Then I'd say this right here is really going to rile his guts." Fadden deftly pulled his pistol and fired a shot through Tandy's stomach.

But Tandy, at the last moment, had seen what was coming, and he fired off one barrel of the shotgun in tandem with Fadden's shot. Tandy's shot missed Fadden but squarely hit Juan, the Mexican, in the chest. Juan shrieked and fell from his horse.

Tandy was kicked back by the joint impact of Fadden's bullet and the recoil of the shotgun. He fell supine, moved in the dirt, then was still. Fadden turned the pistol on Keelan, who sat with his mouth open in horror.

"Get down from there, boy. The extra horse is for you."

Keelan climbed down from the seat, then ran as hard as he could away from the riders. Fadden spurred his horse forward, reached Keelan, then kicked him to the earth with the heel of his boot.

He dropped from the saddle, swept the boy up, and carried him to the reserved horse. He deposited him there, and Keelan did not resist, for he saw it would do him no good.

"Boy, I'm sorry about your nigger friend, but he's the one who came out with the shotgun. You saw that yourself."

The other rider, who had dispassionately been watching the wounded Mexican writhe in the dirt until he was still, came to the side of the buckboard. "Contero's dead," he said.

"Leave him lying," Fadden responded. "The Alianza's loss is the buzzards' gain."

Suddenly Keelan grasped the reins, shouted, and jarred his horse into motion. But Fadden's partner got in front of him and blocked the horse.

"Boy, you just ain't cooperative. Now we got to tie you up," Fadden said.

Keelan tried not to cry as Fadden's partner roughly

bound his hands to the saddlehorn with a rawhide strap. Meanwhile, Fadden rode over to Tandy's body and dismounted. He knelt beside the still form, surprised to see Tandy's eyes slowly open and roll over to look blankly at him.

"You gave it a good try, nigger. Now I got one last job for you. You hang on to this," he said, reaching into his pocket and pulling out an envelope. "If you can't get back to the house, just keep it in your paw. They'll find it when they scoop up your corpse. Bye now."

Fadden stood and mounted again. By now Keelan was well bound, and the other man had tied Juan Contero's horse at the back of Keelan's. "That ought to keep you from running off," the man said with satisfaction.

Fadden nodded his approval. "Mighty fine, then. Let's head to Serveto."

Chapter 3

"Tried to stop them . . . tried to stop them," Tandy said again and again as he lay dying. That he had made it back to the ranch house at all was remarkable, for his wound was severe, and by the time he had somehow driven the buckboard back to the house, its seat was drenched in gore.

Orion knelt by his father's bed, holding the bloody hand, tears streaming down Orion's face. "Tried to stop them," Tandy said again. He turned his face toward the wall, muttered a word in Spanish, and died.

Orion buried his face in the covers.

Brice, standing behind him, bowed his head. He still held the bloodstained note Tandy had brought home with him. All this was too much for Brice to accept—Tandy gunned down, Keelan kidnapped. And upstairs, Garth Kensington himself lay ready to die. Brice had told Kensington of the kidnapping as gently as he could, but it had struck down the old man like a hard kick from a mule. Now Brice did not expect his father-in-law ever to rise from his bed again.

Brice pulled the sheet over Tandy's face and touched Orion's shoulder. "I'm sorry," he said. He turned and walked out of the room, down the stairs, and into Kensington's office.

There he opened and read again the ransom note, written in a scrawled hand:

"Garth Kensington, we got your grandson. For one quarter of a million dollars you can have him back agin. Send it under a white flag by way of his pa and no other to

the Serveto mission within twelve days from now and let
there be no rangers and no law at all or the boy will be kilt at
once. This is no bluff. Bring the cash money to Serveto and
wait with no trickery and we will pick it up and give you back
the boy safe. Send good cash money and we say agin, let
there be no law."

"Serveto," Brice said to himself. He went to the fireplace and burned the note.

The door opened. It was Felipe Espego, Kensington's
gardener.

"Señor James," Felipe said, "there is a man outside to
see Señor Kensington about cattle. What should I tell him?"

Blast, Brice thought. There could be no worse time for
an outsider to arrive. "Tell him Mr. Kensington is ill. Tell him
he has a disease that can be spread, and he has to be kept
away from everyone until he is well. If he asks for me, say I
am away, and let him leave a note. Tell him anything that will
get him away from here, and do the same with everyone else
who comes until I tell you otherwise."

"Sí, señor." The servant withdrew.

Outside, the night shouldered down against the horizon.

They dug Tandy's grave by moonlight and buried him in
a pine box.

At the graveside, Brice looked up at the lighted window
beyond which Garth Kensington lay on his deathbed and
pondered the peculiar twists of life: a man once wealthy and
envied, with abundant power at his command, now lay near
death without enough money to pay even a fraction of the
ransom demand for his own grandson. The kidnappers, of
course, could not know that; they doubtlessly believed
Kensington could pull a quarter of a million dollars from his
back pocket.

That was why, Brice mentally noted, it was essential to
keep Kensington's financial and physical conditions secret.
The kidnappers must have no hint that anything was amiss in
the Kensington dynasty, or else they might abort their plans
and kill Keelan.

Brice and the little cluster of servants buried Tandy,

prayed over the grave, then returned to the house. The servants were silent and tense; once inside, they looked at Brice, waiting for direction.

The meagerness of the group of servants struck Brice. Only five of them. At one time Kensington had kept a dozen servants bustling around his estate, ordering them here and there like a gruff straw boss. No more. His crew of cowpunchers was likewise reduced, though so far Brice and Kensington had been able to explain that away without raising substantial suspicions of financial difficulties. The process of going broke, Brice had learned, makes men into very clever liars.

Brice poured a glass of wine for each servant. He told them all to sit in the drawing room, and pacing before them with his uneven gait, he addressed them.

"For the sake of my son's life, I'm counting on your silence about all of this for now," he said. "So far no one outside those of us in this room knows what has happened, and it must stay that way. The story must be that Mr. Kensington is sick and in isolation, but in no way can we allow even the suspicion he is in danger of his life.

"The kidnapping itself must be kept secret, especially from the law. I have read the ransom note and destroyed it. I know what it demands and how I have to respond. It requires me to leave here for a time. That means these secrets are in your hands. Felipe, I entrust this into your charge for the sake of Keelan."

Felipe nodded, then asked, "Is the ransom large? Will you pay it?"

Brice's throat went dry. He felt a strange urge to tell the truth. Instead he nodded and lied again. "I will pay the ransom. It is large, but we can cover the cost of it."

"Then you will need help to deliver it—guards, gunmen to protect you," Orion Jones said.

"So it would seem. Unfortunately, the kidnappers have not allowed that option."

"But if even a rumor gets out about this, somebody's going to try to steal this ransom from you before it can be delivered."

"I am aware of that. That is why there must be no rumors. None at all. You understand?"

"*Sí*, Señor Brice. We do. But what of you? How can you do this alone?"

Brice turned his back to them. He thought, if I can ride fast enough, if I can find Simon, then I won't be alone, God willing.

When Simon Caine first saw Drew Strahan, he realized the man hadn't lost any of his impressive girth since the war. In fact, Strahan was significantly bigger than before. Caine had to squelch a smile as he watched Strahan spread himself like a blob of half-melted butter across the bench against a wall of his lonely adobe dwelling.

"Most times it's hotter than perdition down here, Simon. Upwards of a hunert in the day, and then cold at night. Ain't right. Something wrong about this here country."

"Then why do you stay?" Caine asked.

Strahan swatted a fly on his neck, then studied the insect's remains on the fleshy heel of his hand. "Because it's a good country in other ways," he said. "If a man puts up with a few scorpions and rattlers, minds his own business, stays halfway honest, and don't bother the rangers or the bandidos, nobody bothers him much, neither. That's been my experience, leastways."

Strahan's house mirrored the crude and slapdash ways of its owner. The adobe structure was dimly lit, dust filled, malodorous—yet it seemed a place where a man was welcome, where he could relax in safety and calm. A sanctuary such as Caine seldom found.

Strahan seemed an unlikely West Texas frontier dweller, with his thoroughly Alabamian accent and his lazy style of living. The broad-jowled, big-lipped man had been a Confederate irregular and sometime bushwhacker during the war, and had come to Texas when it all was over.

Strahan stretched and scratched like an old hound and asked, "Where you heading, Simon?"

"Serveto. I got wind that somebody there was asking for me."

Strahan's expression became serious. "Neal Seahorn?"

"So I was told. For years I hear Seahorn is dead, then comes this letter. Intrigued me a little. I suppose that was one of about three things that led me down here."

"What are the other two?"

"Seeing you is one. The other is my brother, James. Calls himself Brice James now, and lives at the Kensington spread up to the north. Him being my brother is a secret, by the way, so don't talk of it. He's always been ashamed of being linked to an old outlaw like me. And to tell you the truth, when I looked him up, he wasn't too happy to see me. But I don't want to cause him no trouble."

"That's hard, having your own kin turn on you. But I want to know more about Seahorn. How'd you hear he was looking for you?"

"It was all a bit peculiar, Drew. I was staying in a boarding house up in Wichita, calling myself Robert Cole like I do sometimes. I'd just come off a few odd jobs and had a little money. Then I got a letter, addressed to Robert Cole, and it's from Seahorn. What I can't figure is how Seahorn knew my false name and where to find me."

Strahan pursed his thick lips. "What I can't figure is why you'd come answering it. Have you forgotten what Seahorn did to us at Murfreesboro?"

"We never really knew he'd done it, Drew. I'm still not convinced of it."

Strahan snorted. "Well, I am. It was his job to guard for us, but he just kept quiet and let the bluebellies ride in. I believe they paid him off. We almost got killed because of him."

"He said they knocked him in the head."

"I never saw no lumps. Did you?"

"No. But don't forget, Drew—Neal Seahorn nearly took a bullet intended for me later on. I feel like I owe him at least a meeting to hear him out. He says he's going to offer me some kind of job."

"Steer clear of Seahorn, Simon. He's not to be trusted. Besides, he's tied into something big and loco."

"What do you mean?"

"I mean big crime with big connections. And folks who won't let old wars die."

Simon smiled. "That's clear as black coffee, Drew."

"Simon, think for a minute. You just now were wondering how Seahorn knew where to get that letter to you. Him in Mexico, you in Kansas—but still he traced you down. And I know how: through connections he's got to an organization with eyes and ears all over the country. I don't know all that much about it except it's called the Alianza and is led by people with lots of money and lots more old grudges. Old Confederate supporters who never forgave the bluebellies for beating us, and who figure they have the right to gouge what they can out of them now."

"Is Seahorn the leader of this—what did you call it?"

"Alianza. Mex talk for 'alliance.' Seahorn's just one grain in the powder keg. The thing is huge, Simon. I hear it goes right into the government itself. We know it was big enough to track down Simon Caine when the bluebelly government never could. Chew that over for a while before you ride in to see Seahorn."

"How do you know so much about it, Drew? You involved?"

"No, sir. I just got ears that are a little too big and hear a little too well. I'm close enough to Serveto to hear the whispers." He leaned forward. "Steer clear, Simon. When you talk Alianza, you're talking train robberies, bank robberies, kidnapping, extortion. Maybe even assassinations. You're about to get tangled up in something too loco to handle."

"Hang it, Drew. I've dodged the government and the law for years. I can hold my own. Besides, I can always just hear Seahorn out and tell him no thanks."

"Maybe not. The Alianza is like a spiderweb: touch it and you're stuck. Anyone who learns about it is a threat unless he's part of it. So it's best not to hear anything."

"You've obviously heard about it, Drew. And nobody's slit your throat for it."

"That's because I play dumb real well. I don't repeat what I hear—except to an old friend I'm trying to keep out of trouble."

Caine thought it over. "I got to at least hear him out, Drew. I owe Neal Seahorn that much."

Strahan nodded balefully. "All right. Do what you want, Simon. You always were too stubborn to reason with. Just remember that old Drew Strahan warned you."

"That I will."

The top rim of the rising sun had just edged the horizon in fire when Brice put boot in stirrup and slung himself into the saddle of Kensington's best gelding. Booted at his thigh was a gleaming 1873 Winchester rifle, and high on his right hip hung an 1878 Colt single-action Army revolver. His saddlebags were laden with provisions, and he had just finished securing the pack on a second horse he would take with him.

Brice made a final check outside the stable and mounted. He looked at the house, then across the wide plains, where the wind already was stirring up clouds of dust.

Brice was about to ride away when someone called his name. He turned.

Orion Jones walked up to him.

"Don't go just yet. I ain't quite ready."

"Ready for what?"

"I'm going with you."

Brice firmly shook his head. "No, you're not. It's my boy they kidnapped, and my problem."

"And it was my father they shot down like a dog."

"I know that. But what I got to do I got to do alone."

Orion eyed the bundle on the packhorse's back, obviously thinking it contained money. "You go alone with that and you'll be killed."

Brice risked a little honesty. "I don't plan to be alone for long. There's a man who can help me—if he will. The best man I can think of if this thing comes down to shooting and killing. Which it will."

"Who is it?"

"Can't say."

Orion was silent a moment, his mind working. The perception evidenced by his next question surprised Brice.

"Mr. Brice, are you planning to get Keelan back without paying the ransom?"

Brice looked at the handsome black face. "Orion, can you keep one more secret?"

"You know I can."

"There is no ransom. Mr. Kensington is broke. Dead broke. If I get Keelan back, it will have to be through sneaking him out or shooting him out of Serveto."

"Serveto? That's where they took him?"

"Apparently so."

Orion whistled in awe. "I've heard whispers lately—they say the old Serveto mission's occupied again. Bad men. Really bad."

"I've heard the same. I got to go. Don't follow me. You hear?"

Brice was about to ride away, but he stopped. "Orion, right before he died, Tandy said something I couldn't quite make out. Sounded Spanish—"

"I remember. It was *ali-* something. *Alienza*, maybe. Or *alianza*."

"*Alianza*. I wonder why Tandy would say that?"

"I don't know."

Brice turned the gelding and loped off. Orion watched him diminish into the scrubby undergrowth that stretched as far as he could see.

"Serveto," Orion said to himself. He turned and walked back toward the house.

Chapter 4

Puerta de Serveto was a narrow gap in limestone walls beyond which stood the old Serveto mission and presidio. The former was a long-abandoned fortress of the Catholic faith, the latter a fortress for an armed garrison established to protect the mission. Together, the mission and presidio were a crucible in which the culture and religion of New Spain had been protected and nurtured a century before.

Caine was impressed by the size of the old compound. Except for its distinctly Spanish architecture, it reminded him of pictures he had seen in boyhood of ancient European castles surrounded by the hovels of peasants.

He viewed the scene as he descended from the natural rock gateway. The mission and the presidio had been separate but now were joined by a third, middle section made of log and stone walls. The entire tripartite enclosure stood in the center of town, if town this jumble of crude huts could be called. Numerous buildings were visible over the top of the wall—a virtual town within the town. Somewhere inside this old enclosure Caine expected to find Neal Seahorn.

Caine rode through the farrago of poor huts that surrounded Serveto, drawing stares from hollow-eyed women and children in the dirt yards and unpaved streets. He wondered who these people were, and how they managed to eke out a living in this destitute place.

He stopped at a water trough to let his horse refresh itself. An old woman was cranking a windlass at a nearby well. He asked her for a drink, and she handed him the bucket.

The water was cool. He let the water run across his beard and down his neck, soaking his shirt.

He handed the bucket back to the woman, then pointed at the mission. "Seahorn?" he asked.

The woman's eyes grew wide and she quickly turned away. It was as good as an answer—better, for it told Caine something about Seahorn beyond confirming where he could be found. It told him that the people outside the walls were afraid of the man.

Caine mounted and rode toward the front gate of the mission. Atop the wall, a sentry wearing a sombrero and bandolier watched him intently. The brim of the man's sombrero moved in the hot breeze as he paced.

The front gate was closed and barred, so Caine rode to a spot nearby, dismounted, and sat down in the shade of a tree. A boy selling melons passed; Caine bought a slice and ate it. Tilting his hat down over his forehead, he dozed.

"*Señor.*"

He lifted his hat. A tall Mexican stood above him. Dressed finely, the man was lean and well-groomed. His mustache was trimmed to a thin line above his straight lips. His skin was very brown, his hair curly and closely cropped.

"Señor Caine, I am Ramon Fernandez. I saw you from the east wall. We have been expecting you."

"You're with Seahorn?"

"*Sí.* You will accompany me inside?"

The massive gate opened to them, and they passed through, Caine leading his Appaloosa. He wrinkled his nose at the crazy mix of stenches that struck him inside the enclosure: horse and chicken dung, molds, dust, hay, meat, and cookstove smoke heavy with the smell of hot Mexican spices.

Within the enclosure stood dirty adobe buildings with *vigas* jutting in a row above low doorways, *ristras* of chili peppers hanging from them in scarlet strings. Here and there around the walls stood pens filled with livestock, or with chickens that pecked the dusty ground. Lazy dogs roamed about.

The men of Serveto, though, were what drew Caine's attention most. They were a mix of Anglos, Mexicans, Indians, and half-breeds, and all looked seedy and dangerous. They were armed to a man.

"What kind of place is this?" Caine asked as they meandered through the bustle.

"Once a place of religion. Now a place of something very different," Ramon said. "For more than a hundred years these walls have stood here. It is a good place for Neal Seahorn's purpose."

"Which is?"

Ramon smiled. His teeth were white and straight. "I speak too much. You will know soon enough."

"Where does Seahorn live?"

Ramon pointed toward a building in the center of the plaza. It probably had been the quarters of priests at some time past, Caine guessed. Two wide double doors stood open at the building's base. Two levels of balconies stretched across its front, with full-length, arch-topped windows leading out to them through the stone wall.

"Behind the center window is Seahorn's quarters. I suspect he watches us from there even now."

"Why doesn't he come down to meet me?"

"Seahorn seldom leaves his chambers now. He has reasons, I suppose. You will meet him later in those chambers."

"Who are all the folk here?"

"These within the walls are the followers of Neal Seahorn, and their families, if they have them. Many of those outside the walls fear those of us in here, but they come to us for the protection we offer."

"Protection from what? The law?"

"You are perceptive, Señor Caine. Come now. It is not yet time for you to go to Seahorn. He wishes to meet you under his own circumstances. So we will go now and enjoy a drink, eh?"

They went to a cantina in a back corner of the enclosure. Caine tethered his horse in the shade of a heat-stunted tree, and he and Ramon walked inside. Cool and rather dark, the cantina was clean and pleasant. They found a corner table.

"How long have you worked for Seahorn, Ramon?" Caine asked when they had tequila in hand.

Ramon shook his head. "I do not work for any man but myself," he said. "I merely sell my services to whoever pays me the price I demand. At the moment that is Neal Seahorn."

"Your services?"

Ramon nodded and tapped the butt of his pistol with a long forefinger. Caine had figured as much.

"So when will Seahorn be ready to see me?" Caine asked.

"Tonight, *amigo*. For now let us drink."

His hair was gray as gun steel, his eyes sparkling blue. Neal Seahorn still had the muscled build of a much younger man, but his shoulders were beginning to stoop, and in his blue eyes was a hint of deep weariness.

He stood in the arch-topped window of his quarters, looking out over the balcony to the enclosed plaza. A crescent rim of the declining sun shone over the wall, casting an orange glow and long shadows across the plaza. A sentry paced below, and a man with a bottle weaved and staggered across the plaza, singing loudly in Spanish.

Seahorn turned away from the window and swept his eyes across his lamplit room.

Quite a contrast it was to the squalor outside. There were paintings on the wall, a fine oak sideboard, two overstuffed chairs, a long table spread with food—roast duck, boiled potatoes, rice, fresh bread—American dishes, not the overspiced Mexican swill Seahorn had reluctantly become accustomed to since coming to Serveto more than a year ago. This was a special meal for a special guest.

Seahorn rubbed his hands together, then smiled self-consciously. He was surprisingly tense. It had been many years since he had seen Simon Caine, and the prospect of meeting him made him nervous.

To relax himself, he poured a glass of wine and sat down. A tall clock in the corner ticked off two more minutes. There was a knock on the door. Seahorn quickly drained off his glass.

"Enter," he called.

The door swung open. Ramon stood in the center of the doorway, his ready smile flashing. Caine was behind him, indistinct in the shadows. Seahorn waved them inside.

"Simon," Seahorn said. "Too many years since I've seen you, my friend."

Caine nodded. His unreadable eyes evaluated Seahorn head to toe. "You haven't changed much," Caine said succinctly.

Seahorn smiled. "You flatter me. The years leave tracks on us all. But you look well—you always were a handsome man, whether you realized it or not."

"Never gave it any thought."

Seahorn waved his hand toward the table. "In your honor, Simon. A meal I think you will appreciate. We have important things to discuss, and discussion is better when the belly is full." He turned to Ramon. "Thank you, my friend."

Ramon departed. Caine took off his hat. His eye fell on Seahorn's empty wineglass.

"A drink for you, Simon? Some wine? Tequila?"

"Got whiskey?"

"I should have remembered—Simon Caine relishes good whiskey." Seahorn took a bottle from a cabinet and poured Caine an amber-colored shot. He took more wine for himself, then he and Caine talked quietly and drank. Seahorn was as tense as Caine was calm. After a few minutes and another drink they sat down to eat.

The meal was as good as it looked. Caine was ravenous and ate heartily. Seahorn ate with tense dignity, often dabbing his napkin on his lips. A Mexican girl came in and out several times, carrying in full bowls, carrying out empty ones.

"I heard you were shot down by *federales* in Chihuahua, Neal," Caine said.

"It was a widespread story, and as useful as it was false. I went away for many years. Just vanished. I fell in with a wise old Mexican man I met in a cantina near El Paso—Old Pablo, he called himself—and for years we rode together. He virtually became my father. Then other things just drew me away.

Old Pablo lives alone now down near the bend of the Rio Bravo. Someday I'll go back and get him, take him somewhere far from this country, and give him the kind of last days every man ought to have."

The conversation drifted to the war. Seahorn spoke of it like a man talking of a lost-but-fondly-remembered lover. At last Caine tired of it all, sat back in his chair, and looked Seahorn squarely in the eye.

"What do you want with me, Neal?"

Seahorn dabbed his lips again and poured himself another glass of wine. He stood and walked to the window with his back to Caine.

"Do you think often of the war, Simon?"

It seemed a foolish question, and Caine did not answer foolish questions.

"I know you do," Seahorn went on. "You and I will never forget those days. Neither will many others. But there are those of us who remember more, and more deeply, eh? Who never forget and never turn away."

"What's your point?"

Seahorn turned. His expression was more intense than before, as if a mask had been removed. He suddenly was more like the Neal Seahorn Caine had known during the old bushwhacking days. It was a funny thing: Caine recalled only now how obsessive Seahorn had been at times, how reckless.

"Have you ever heard of the Alianza, Simon?"

"A whisper or two."

Seahorn sat down at the table again and leaned forward. "The war is over, Simon. I know that. But it is a fire that still smolders. And even a smoldering fire can cast off a few sparks, eh? Maybe even enough to burn those who wander too close. That's what the Alianza is all about."

"I don't know what you're talking about."

"Then hear me out for a moment. Let me describe the Alianza. It . . . we . . . are a secret group. We talk little of ourselves, and there are many who disbelieve in us. And that is fine, for it makes what we do all the easier."

"And what is that?"

"The bluebelly government would call it crime. The

Alianza calls it the due of those who lost a war they should have won. The Alianza believes that even a snake that is trodden upon can at least bite the heel of the treader. That is what we're doing: biting the heel of the Yankee government. In the process we are taking all we can from its corrupt system—its banks, its trains, its freight lines. We of the Alianza are from the bluebelly viewpoint organized criminals— thieves, counterfeiters, extortionists, kidnappers. From our own viewpoint we are merely taking, in whatever way we can, the good life that was wrongly denied us at Appomattox."

"This whole fortress, all these men—they are part of the Alianza?"

"A small part of it. A few ants in a hill bigger than you might imagine. I work for the Alianza, generate money for it, hire men like those around me—and it in turn supports me. Quite well."

"Was it the Alianza who found me for you?"

"Yes. At my request."

"So here I am. What do you want of me?"

"To join me. Become my right hand. It will be lucrative— that I promise. A way I can repay you—"

"Repay?"

Seahorn's eyes flickered down, then back up. "Yes. For what happened in Murfreesboro."

Caine understood. "So it's true—you really did let those bluebellies through?"

"Yes. But I wasn't paid off, no matter what you may have been told. It was fear, Simon. I admit that freely. For fear of my own life I hid when they passed. I couldn't have stopped them. They would have killed me."

"They almost did kill me. And Jake Armitage and Drew Strahan, too."

"Don't you think I know that? The guilt of it will always haunt me."

"Maybe so, but I can't believe that after all this time the only reason you've called me is to even up an old debt. What else do you want from me?"

Seahorn licked lips that had suddenly gone dry. "I want your gun. Your reputation. Your name linked with mine."

"Why?"

Seahorn glanced at the door through which Ramon had departed. "Because I can't trust them anymore. They're turning against me."

"Who?"

"My men. All of them. I'm the captain of a ship of mutineers." Caine noted that Seahorn was actually trembling.

Seahorn went on. "It's not just the men I'm concerned about. It's the Alianza itself. It's turning on me, too."

"Why?"

"I think they're beginning to believe I'm stealing from them. They think I'm skimming off more than my percentage."

"Are you?"

Seahorn forced a chuckle. "What does that matter? The point is they believe I am. I feel them turning against me on one side, while my own men whisper about wealth I'm supposedly hiding. It's becoming a nightmare, and I admit I'm scared."

"And you want me to join your nightmare?"

"You don't understand. With you with me it would be different. People stand in awe of you, Simon. The men here see you as invulnerable, and they respect you. The Alianza would respect you, too. With you beside me they would leave me—us—alone. You would be a cork in the bottleneck, keeping things peaceful for a bit longer. And then very soon we will simply disappear—as very wealthy men. All I need is your presence for a few days until a very large ransom arrives. Part is to go to me, part to the Alianza. But . . ."

Caine finished for him. "But you really plan to keep it all for yourself."

"And for you, if you'll join me. And half of what I've already saved."

"Saved or stolen?" Caine laughed. "A thief stealing from other thieves."

Seahorn's lip twitched and his brows lowered over his eyes. "Don't call me a thief, Simon. I don't like that."

Caine stood. "And I don't like what you're offering me. Sounds like death on a platter. I don't want any part of it."

Seahorn looked incredulous. "You're turning me down?"

"That's right."

Seahorn stood, turning over his glass. "You've leaving me to be killed!" He stopped. "Wait—is this revenge for Murfreesboro? You're betraying me now because I let those Yanks through?"

"This isn't betrayal, and Murfreesboro has nothing to do with it. I just don't want to do it." Caine turned and walked toward the door. "Thanks for the food, Neal. It was prime."

Seahorn went to him, grasped his shoulder. "You can't just walk out on me."

"Let me go."

"They'll kill me."

"Then leave. Get away before they get to you."

Caine jerked loose and turned. He put his hand on the door latch. He sensed quick motion behind him. Instinctively he ducked and turned slightly, but something heavy came down hard on the back of his head. The room spun and he collapsed senseless to the floor.

Chapter 5

Brice found the isolated residence of Drew Strahan only after great difficulty and loss of time. When he was near losing all hope of finding it, an inquiry of a hunter coming up from the Big Bend country at last put him right. But when he reached Strahan's, he received a hostile gunpoint reception.

Brice identified himself as Simon Caine's brother from Kensington. Strahan put his broad face close to Brice's and looked him over with squinted eyes, then nodded slowly.

"I see a lot of Simon in your face," he said. He lowered the pistol. "All right. I believe you. He said he had a brother from Kensington, and you got to be him."

"I'm looking for Simon," Brice said.

"Too late. He's gone."

Brice felt like sinking into the ground. "Where did he go?" he asked.

Strahan looked skeptically at him. "Simon told me you weren't too receptive when he came to see you. Why are you looking for him now?"

Brice told Strahan about the kidnapping and his hope that Simon could somehow help him recover Keelan. He spared no detail, even telling of Garth Kensington's inability to pay the ransom. "I don't know what to do. I've got only a few days before they'll be looking for me to bring the ransom into Serveto," Brice said.

Strahan's eyes narrowed. "Serveto, you say?"

Brice nodded.

"Well, that's exactly where Simon was headed."

"What?"

Strahan told Brice of the Alianza, Neal Seahorn, and his call to Caine to come to Serveto to meet him. Strahan told of his suspicion that Caine was to be invited to join the criminal organization. "But Simon knew nothing about your boy being kidnapped," Strahan said. "If he had, he would never have come here. He would have gone straight to Serveto to take off Neal Seahorn's head."

"So you're saying this Alianza is responsible for the kidnapping?"

"Looks that way to me. It's a crazy twist—Seahorn searching out Simon on the one hand and snatching his nephew on the other."

"What could it mean?"

"I don't know."

"There's no chance Simon will join the Alianza, is there?"

Strahan frowned. "You his brother or not? What do you think?"

Brice said, "I don't think he'd ever join. But that doesn't help me. I got no ransom, and now I don't even have Simon to help me."

Strahan looked sincerely sympathetic. "I'd like to help you myself, son, but this is one old pistol fighter who's too old and eat up with gout to be anything but a hindrance. But what I can offer you right now is a meal and a place to sleep tonight."

"I'm obliged," Brice said. He looked out the door and across the horizon.

"What are you looking at?"

"Nothing. I just thought I saw—" He stopped.

"What?"

What Brice could have said was, I thought I saw a horseman on the horizon. But Brice looked again and saw nothing, and he thought maybe it had been an illusion brought on by fatigue.

"I didn't see anything," Brice said. "Thank you for your help, Mr. Strahan."

        *   *   *

Caine awakened in darkness. He was lying on some soft but lumpy surface, surrounded by looming shapes and black shadows. Pain radiated through his skull, and at the back of his head was a tender place that made him wince when his groping hand touched it.

He lay there a few minutes, trying to make sense of where he was, but he could not. He pushed up on his elbows, then climbed to his knees and finally his feet. He moved slowly, making sure he had no injuries beyond a sore skull.

He almost tripped on his first step. He knelt and felt about him. The soft, lumpy surface on which he had been lying was a heap of old rags and sacks. He investigated the room further. The big shapes around him were crates and casks. Apparently this was some sort of storage chamber.

He found a window and opened its shutters. Moonlight streamed in. The window was crossed with iron bars; no opportunity for escape there.

Caine sat down on a crate and massaged the back of his neck until his head hurt less. His gunbelt was gone. Nothing in his pockets at all—not even matches to light one of the lamps hanging along the wall. All he had was what he had on, and his hat that lay on the floor beside the pile of rags.

He muttered a curse at Neal Seahorn, then another at himself for not having listened to Drew Strahan and stayed away from Serveto.

Caine explored the room. It was about fifty feet square and had a stone-tile floor and a tall ceiling. All three of the room's windows were barred. A wide double door was the only apparent entrance and exit. On the far side of the room a platform had been built for extra storage space, with a ramp leading up to it. There more casks hung in parbuckles, and ropes and pulleys dangled.

Caine went to the double door. He didn't attempt to open it, for he knew it would be barred from the outside. Probably Seahorn had posted a guard out there anyway. Caine listened—a boot scuffed the floor in the hallway; a whiff of tobacco smoke filtered in through the crack between the doors.

Quietly Caine crept to the center of the room, vanishing into the shadows there. He appraised his circumstances.

He couldn't figure what Seahorn had in mind for him. Caine wondered if Seahorn was insane. Much of his talk had sounded obsessive and excessively fearful. Whatever Seahorn's state, it seemed probable that the Alianza was no madman's illusion. Only a big and wealthy entity could support Seahorn and his gunmen in a place and manner such as this.

Caine wished he could smoke but knew he couldn't. He didn't want the guard outside to come in—at least not until he had developed some plan of escape.

Returning to the window, he tried to determine his location. This building appeared to be somewhere toward the center of the enclosure. It was not, as far as he could tell, near the wall on any side. A bad situation. Once out of here, he would have to make it across open space, then find some way to mount and cross the wall without being seen.

The immediate problem, though, was simply getting out of this room. Caine looked around, but no likely options presented themselves.

He slowly walked around the room, trying to plan. He could call in the guard and then try to overcome him, but that was risky. There might be more than one guard, and a scuffle might draw attention from elsewhere in the compound.

Caine explored the main floor again but developed no new ideas.

He heard a noise at the doorway. An Anglo voice said, "Seahorn wants to know if he's stirred yet."

"I've heard nothing," said someone with a Mexican voice. "I'm tired of sitting here. Why can't we just lock him up in the carcel?"

"Seahorn said he wants him treated special. Those two rode together once, you know. Come on. Let's check him out."

After the rattle of a key in a lock, one of the big doors swung open and the two men entered. One carried a lamp. They walked to the pile of rags and sacks in the midst of the jumble of crates and barrels. Caine lay as before, eyes loosely shut, mouth slightly open.

The Anglo man said, "Must have took quite a lick. I would have figured he'd be stirring by now."

"Perhaps he will die," said the Mexican.

The Anglo laughed. "It'd take more than a knock on the head to kill Simon Caine. All I can say is, when he does wake up, Seahorn better keep out of his reach. Caine's twice the man Seahorn is."

"Such talk can get you killed here," the Mexican said.

"I ain't afraid of Seahorn. One of these days I'll swing his scalp from my belt and jingle his money in my pocket."

The men walked away; Caine heard the door shut and the key turn.

He sat up, breathing deeply. He remained seated in the heap of rags, beginning to believe he would have no choice but to try to fight his way out.

He stood and decided to explore one more time before taking that desperate option. He quietly climbed up the ramp to the second level. He noticed a crack in the top of the wall directly across from him. He followed it down with his eyes; it disappeared behind a crate stacked against the wall.

He moved the crate aside inch by inch so as to make no noise. The crack widened here into a hole about the size of a man's head, and at its base it was even wider. Caine lay down on his side and looked out the opening.

Beyond it he saw the dark expanse of a tiled flat roof. The room he was in was two stories high, but apparently the rest of the building was only one story, butting up against the taller portion.

Caine scouted about until he found a scrap of metal. As quietly as he could, he chipped away the crumbling stone around the hole, making the opening bigger. Sweat soaked his shirt, and his head throbbed.

When the hole was big enough, he pushed himself through. It was a tight squeeze, and it took several minutes for him to make it. When he was out, he crouched on the roof and looked across the plaza below.

Light poured out of numerous windows here and there around the compound. Caine heard scraps of conversation, muffled laughter in the wind. These were the sounds of people talking and smoking over tables of food and cards and liquor.

He dropped lightly to the ground, thinking of weapons. He wanted his own back again but had no way to know where Seahorn would have put them, nor if he could reach them.

The sound of footfalls nearby made him slip back against the wall. Still feeling exposed, he dropped to his belly and snaked under a boardwalk just as two men came around the corner. One was an American, a stranger to Caine. The other was Ramon Fernandez.

"No problems then?" Ramon asked.

"None except losing Juan Contero. We rode in, snatched the boy, rode out. Shot up a darky that was with the boy. I figure he's 'gwine cross de ribber' by now." The man laughed.

"Do you foresee problems getting the ransom?"

"None. That old man could pay whatever you ask without a flinch. Sit tight and they'll deliver that ransom right to our door. You just wait."

The men went on, leaving Caine unseen below the boardwalk, evaluating what he had heard. A kidnapping, apparently—undoubtedly the same one from which Seahorn was expecting ransom, as he had mentioned. Part of the Alianza's design that Seahorn found so grand. And the victim apparently just a boy.

It made Caine think about his own long-lost son, and he hated Neal Seahorn.

Chapter 6

Keeping in shadows and doorways, Caine traveled through the enclosure, searching for a way out. He heard someone whistling nearby and sank back into a dark doorway.

A Mexican with a Colt Dragoon hanging butt-forward on a cord against his thigh passed, whistling a tune. He held a jangling key ring in one hand, and a stack of rifles and carbines beneath his arm. He went by Caine without seeing him.

Caine fell in behind the man's path, his eye on the weapons. The man walked to a stone building about two hundred feet away and thrust a key into the lock.

Caine stealthily approached. When the Mexican swung out the door, Caine was right behind him. The Mexican stepped inside, and in a perfectly coordinated move, Caine slammed the heavy door against him. Its timbers pounded the man's head against the doorframe and dropped him cold.

Caine dragged the bulky form into the building and pulled the door nearly shut behind him. He found matches in one of the man's pockets and lit one.

He smiled. This obviously was Seahorn's armory. Rifles and shotguns, ranging from ancient percussion-cap weapons to Winchesters still thick with packing grease, stood racked around the wall. Flat crates held other rifles, most apparently new. Beneath tarpaulins in the corner there were two Gatling guns, and against the wall stood casks of powder, countless packages of bullets, gun-repair equipment, ammunition-manufacturing equipment, and other such goods. There was enough weaponry here to outfit a small army—which, Caine realized, Seahorn's band really was.

Lighting match after match to see by, Caine gathered arms. He took a brand-new Colt six-shooter and all the bullets his pockets would hold, then began looking for a good rifle. He selected a familiar-looking Winchester and suddenly realized that it was his own weapon, the very one he had bought in Missouri to replace the aging weapons he had carried while in the Bitterroots. His old Navy Colt he had never parted with, though, and he began digging about, hoping it had also been stored here. Quickly he was rewarded. The pistol, still loaded, hung in Caine's own gunbelt from a peg on the wall, ammunition pouch intact. Gratefully Caine strapped the belt on. He loaded his new weapons and put fresh loads in the Navy Colt.

Rearmed, Caine cautiously left the hut and darted across the clearing to a double row of flat-topped adobe houses, or casas, near the west wall. There he mulled what to do next.

Suddenly, as if at some silent signal, the compound exploded in a burst of activity, and Caine knew his escape had finally been detected.

Someone on the other side of the enclosure shouted something indiscernible in Spanish. Caine dropped to his belly. He heard his own name amid the flurry of words.

Lights flickered on here and there, and men emerged from doorways. Dogs barked. Caine began snaking off toward the compound wall, his rifle in front of him. Someone ran by not twenty feet from him but did not see him. Caine reached the corner of the row of adobes and stood in a crouch.

A grove of trees around a well at the corner of the compound appeared to be the most promising hiding place within view. Caine darted toward it. But he saw a man with a rifle slightly to the right of it, and he had to fall back again into the alley between the rows of adobe dwellings.

The man appeared to be searching. Caine waited impatiently until he had meandered off. More shouts erupted in the center of the compound as Caine stepped out again, heading toward the well and the dark trees.

"*Señor.*"

It was a lady's voice, spoken from no more than six feet away. He wheeled and instinctively raised his rifle.

A dark-haired figure, unmistakably feminine, stood in the open window just to his right.

"They will find you if you do not hide," the lady said. "Come in. Quickly!"

Footfalls, shouts—men approaching.

Caine hesitated only a moment. Then he climbed into the Mexican woman's dark house through the window, and she drew the shutters closed behind him.

She took Caine to a back room full of crockery jars, churns, water bottles, and bundles of kindling tied with twine. He hid among the latter, pulling bundles atop himself. He lay as still as possible, trying not to breathe too loudly.

He fully realized that he might have thrown his life away by trusting this dark-eyed stranger. He had entered her house because his instincts told him to, and because he had no better alternative.

"They will come here, Señor Caine, and ask for you," she said in a low voice. *She knows my name*, Caine noted. "I will lie to them and turn them away."

He heard voices and footfalls outside, then the violent opening of the door. A thick Mexican voice fired out a string of questions and demands. The woman talked back, sounding afraid.

Men moved through the house; Caine heard doors opened, furniture moved—then someone was in the room with him.

Caine peered carefully up through the kindling. A tall Mexican with dark braids about his ears was peering about the little room, pistol drawn. Caine steeled himself, but suddenly the Mexican turned away, his braids flapping from the quick motion. He said something to the lady that Caine could not understand, then laughed roughly; Caine somehow got an impression that he had also touched her improperly. Then the front door opened and closed. He heard the men retreating, then silence. Caine pushed the kindling bundles aside and rose.

She was at the door. She was a strikingly beautiful

woman, wearing black. "Why are you doing this?" Caine asked. "How do you know my name?"

"I am Rosalita Contero," she said. "I help you because I hear you have offended the swine Seahorn. He is an evil man, so if you have angered him, you must be good. Everyone here knows who you are, *señor*. The talk of you has been everywhere."

"If you despise this place so, why do you stay?"

"My husband was Juan Contero, a *secuestrador* . . . how you say?—a kidnapper for Seahorn. Now it has cost him his life. Do not say you are sorry—it was the justice of God against a bad man I was fool enough to love." She crossed herself and touched a crucifix about her neck. "I will go soon, and spit upon my memories of Serveto and Neal Seahorn."

Caine said, "I got to get over the wall. And I need a horse."

"Hide again for now. I will tell you when it is safe."

She buried Caine beneath the kindling again. He lay there a long time. He heard her stirring about, poking a fire, brewing something in a kettle. Then, after what seemed more than an hour, she returned. She had a shawl over her shoulders.

"There is small door through the west wall," she said. "It is hidden by vines and was covered over with bricks, but for now it is exposed again. The children have done it in play only this week, and the men here have not yet seen it." She gave Caine a poncho and a sombrero. "These will help disguise you."

The compound was bathed in darkness. A thin sliver of moon sailed into and out of intermittent clouds, its sporadic light watery and pale. Caine walked beside Rosalita, keeping his weapons hidden beneath the faded poncho. The hat was too large and rode low on his forehead.

Men still moved about the compound, rifles in hand. They looked in doorways, under wagons, in brush, but without the sense of urgency evident before. Caine and Rosalita walked with deliberate slowness toward a dark alley between two buildings ahead.

"Rosalita!"

Caine winced at the sound of the voice. "Go on," Rosalita whispered. "Do not stop for anything. The door is there, beneath the vines..."

"Rosalita!" Now Caine recognized the coarse voice. That of the big Mexican man with the braids.

Rosalita, pretending to have heard only the second call, turned. Caine continued on, into the alleyway, then stopped in the shadows and watched Rosalita as the big man approached her. He was a mountain, dwarfing her. He grinned, leaning toward her; his hands groped lewdly. Rosalita slapped at him and he laughed. But suddenly his body spasmed as Caine's rifle stock pounded into the back of his skull. The Mexican collapsed, shuddering spasmodically into senselessness.

Rosalita upbraided Caine for returning. "You are loco! You will be seen!"

"I couldn't stand by and watch him do that."

Caine and Rosalita hurried into the alley together. They rounded the back of one of the adobe buildings. Rosalita pulled aside some vines on an old arbor and exposed a small, arch-shaped door that long ago had been bricked and mortared over. But as Rosalita had said, the mortar and bricks had pulled away; they lay heaped behind the arbor vines and before the outward-opening door.

"Once there was a mission granary here, and this door opened to it from the outside," she said. "Those of us who know it is open again say nothing. I will leave through it myself as soon as I have the last pay that was to go to my husband." She looked ashamed. "It is evil money, I know, but yet I must have it."

"I understand. I'm obliged to you, Rosalita," Caine said. "Don't know how to thank you."

"Perhaps someday you will help me, *Dios mediante*," she said. "Now go. Across the hill to the north Seahorn keeps stables—there you can steal a horse. Ride swift and far, Simon Caine."

She closed the door. Simon loped away into the night, the wide brim of his sombrero flapping.

*   *   *

At Seahorn's stables a campfire burned brightly in the wind, and silhouetted in it Caine saw a seated guard holding a carbine.

Caine strode up to him. "Hello!" he called. The man leaped up, turning, lifting the carbine.

"Whoa, there!" Caine said, laughing in apparent good nature. "No need to get jumpy. Just wanted to buy a horse. How you Mexes say it—*compra caballo*—or something like that?"

The man levered the carbine warningly. Caine put on a mask of fear. He lifted his hands. "Please, *amigo*. Don't shoot me. I am a sick and weak man. I . . . I . . ." Suddenly he clutched at his chest, groaned, and fell prone.

The man with the carbine peered cautiously at Caine, then edged forward. Caine did not move. The man rolled him over. Caine swung up his pistol and cracked the butt into the side of the man's head. The man fell atop him, and Caine pushed him off. Caine was up in half a moment. But the man was not unconscious. He raised the carbine. Caine kicked it away, then followed up with a second kick, this to the man's chin. The guard did not move.

Caine levered the shells out of the carbine, tossed it into a manure stack, and entered the corral, looking for a good mount. He thanked good fortune that nobody from the compound was yet here looking for him; perhaps they still figured him to be inside the walls, hiding.

Caine grinned when he saw his own Appaloosa. He claimed it and led it to the stable, where he furiously searched for his saddle. He found it hanging over the side of a stall. Caine quickly saddled the Appaloosa, booted his weapons, and mounted.

He heard a shout from somewhere, then a shot. A bullet passed a foot above his head. He bent low. A sentry on the compound's wall had spotted him.

Caine rode into a night-shadowed street lined by crude huts. He whipped the Appaloosa into a run when he heard noise behind him. He saw dark faces peer at him from behind doors and glassless windows, but from these silent people he had nothing to fear.

Near the edge of the cluster of hovels he cut right, riding

into a black alley between two apparently deserted buildings. There he dismounted and with his weight worked the Appaloosa to the ground. He hid behind its heaving form.

A few moments later a band of riders flashed by the end of the alley, riding on past and out of town. Caine smiled and rose. The Appaloosa struggled to its feet.

"*Señor.*"

Caine spun. The big Mexican with the twin braids stood behind him, about fifteen feet away, grinning. He had followed Caine. In his hand was a Colt six-shooter. Blood was drying on his head.

Caine drew his pistol just as the Mexican's fat finger began its squeeze on the trigger. Two guns fired as one. The braided Mexican's shot winged inches past Caine and his mount. But Caine's own shot punched a hole through the Mexican's broad belly, and the man fell dead.

"That one was for you, Rosalita," Caine said.

He mounted and pushed the Appaloosa into the wilderness east of Serveto, knowing that the shots would quickly draw back the riders and he would be pursued.

Seahorn's face was livid. It lent him a wild, ghastly look that Ramon Fernandez had seldom seen.

"He has made me a fool before my own men, and before the Alianza itself," Seahorn said. "Go find him. Bring him back to me. Alive, if possible."

"Indeed."

Ramon left Seahorn and walked through the compound. Against the west wall stood a sort of barracks building where priests once had lived. A larger building stood across from them. Long ago it had been a mission school, but now it was the jail, or carcel, of Neal Seahorn.

Ramon walked to its doorway. A sentinel stood to the side and let him pass.

J. W. Fadden was inside, seated on a bench beside a heavy oak door.

"The boy?" Ramon asked.

"In there."

"Let me see him."

Fadden stood and lifted the bar of the door. He swung it inward, and he and Ramon entered.

A miniature tornado broke loose inside the room. Keelan, flailing and kicking, almost knocked Ramon to the floor, then darted past him for the doorway.

Fadden's arm swept out and caught Keelan by the neck. Fadden pulled the boy back against him.

"Ain't polite to run out on your friends," Fadden said.

Keelan gurgled and choked, struggling for his breath.

Ramon leaned over, examining Keelan as if he were a colt being considered for purchase.

"He looks ill," Ramon said. "Make sure he gets plenty to eat and drink. A corpse brings no *dinero*."

"I'm no nursemaid," Fadden said flatly.

Ramon looked at Fadden with undisguised contempt. Fadden, who couldn't care less, picked up Keelan and roughly tossed him on his cot.

"My pa will come here, and he'll kill you," Keelan said, fighting tears. "My grandpa, too—he's old, but he's got a lot of money and he can make you pay!"

"Wrong, boy—we're making him pay, or else he gets you back one piece at a time," Fadden said.

Ramon said, "There is no need to talk to a mere *muchacho* in such a way."

"Just being truthful."

"Neal Seahorn wants you to be useful instead. Go saddle up. I am gathering men to go after Simon Caine."

"Caine got loose?" Fadden chuckled admiringly. "That explains the ruckus."

"Yes. Now go."

Fadden slowly turned and walked out, his carelessly stooped shoulders rolling with his gait. At the door he turned. "Mexican man, watch your mouth around me from here on out. A lot here see you as Seahorn's servant boy, and when they finally turn on him, you'll be the first to chew a bullet." He smiled coldly. "Maybe it will be mine."

Ramon smiled. "I will see any such effort as a welcome opportunity for reciprocation, *amigo*."

Fadden looked defiant but puzzled. Ramon laughed, for he knew that Fadden had not understood the meaning of what he had just heard. Fadden stalked out.

Keelan looked up at Ramon. "Will you let me go free, mister?"

Ramon merely smiled, rubbed the boy's head. "Be patient, *muchacho*, and say your prayers. Perhaps heaven will open and take you in." He laughed and rubbed Keelan's head again. The boy pulled away.

Ramon left the room and locked the door behind him.

Chapter 7

Drew Strahan squeezed shut his eyes until they were mere slits in his sweating brown face. Supine, he gritted his teeth and tried not to cry out as the bearded, derby-wearing man who held the Peacemaker to his throat once again ground the heel of his riding boot into his gout-racked ankle.

"Again, Mr. Strahan," said the man, whose name was Morrison Deguere, "why did Brice James come here?"

"I'll . . . kill you . . ."

"I think not. Now talk, so I can get out of here before I lose him." Deguere almost sadly shook his head as he bore down with his heel again, for he disliked distasteful things. But he disliked uncooperative old men even more.

Strahan groaned, yelled, then relented. "Mexico! He went into Mexico."

Deguere eased up only a bit. "Exactly where?"

"Serveto. Serveto."

"Why did he come here first?"

Strahan blubbered, hating himself for talking. "He came because he thought somebody might be here."

"Who?"

Strahan clenched his teeth. Deguere bore down until his victim screamed.

"Simon Caine. He was looking for Simon Caine."

"Who I happen to know is Brice James's brother," Deguere said, nodding. "Just what I suspected. Why was he searching for Caine now?"

"Needs his help."

"Go on."

Strahan hung his head. "Brice James's boy got kid-napped. By Neal Seahorn's men, I think. Brice came hoping to find Simon and get him to help get the boy back."

Deguere looked fascinated; this interrogation was prov-ing worth the trouble. "Does Caine know about the kidnapping?"

Strahan was hurting and his voice sounded tight. "Didn't when he was here."

"So Caine really was here? Where did he go?"

"Serveto. He was answering a call from Neal Seahorn. That's all I know. Who are you? Why are you asking all this?"

"That doesn't matter. Do you know much about the Alianza?"

Strahan looked scared now. "I've heard the name. I don't know what it is."

"I believe you do—your eyes show it. Tell me, was Caine prepared to join the Alianza?"

Strahan bit his lip, not wanting to talk. Deguere pressed again on the ankle.

"No! No. Simon just had his mind set on hearing Seahorn out. I told him not to go, but he wouldn't listen."

"Fascinating. Absolutely fascinating." Deguere lifted his foot off the tortured ankle, which Strahan immediately seized and began rubbing. "So what is Brice James going to do about his kidnapped boy?" Deguere asked.

"He's going to try to get him out alone."

"With ransom?"

"He's got no ransom. Garth Kensington's gone broke, he says." Strahan looked at Deguere with blurry eyes. "Are you from the Alianza? How do you know who I am?"

"Just count me as one who has good reason to know all I can about Simon Caine and his old partners, yourself includ-ed. I've been on Caine's trail for a long time now. I could recite a history of his life and associations in great detail. I could even tell you much about yourself, Mr. Strahan." He shifted the derby and looked ponderingly at the other. "Now the question is what to do with you, my friend. What indeed?"

Strahan squeezed his eyes shut. He cried out when the

Peacemaker blasted. Half a minute later he opened his eyes. He was unscathed. The bearded man had fired into the floor near Strahan's head, then had left. The deliberately inaccurate shot was a final cruel jest, a mercy for himself as a traitor that somehow hurt almost as much as a bullet would have.

Strahan put his face to the floor and lay there a long time.

Morrison Deguere sat beneath a rock, letting his horse drink at a seep and graze at the meager grasses growing around it. Deguere was eager to go on and further close the gap between himself and Brice James, but the horse was nearly exhausted. So, pencil in hand, Deguere brushed his fingers through his beard and flipped a page in his black notebook. The book held the record of more than a year of tracking Simon Caine, starting when Deguere left Henley in the Montana Territory under the hire of Caine's old enemy, William Montrose, brother of the man who had killed Caine's family in Tennessee and then had died at Caine's hand.

Montrose had hired Deguere because of his reputation as one of the most capable detectives available west of New York. Deguere's assignment was simple: trail Simon Caine as long as it takes to bring him down.

It was the kind of assignment Deguere relished. The federal government had never been able to bring in Caine, but that didn't worry him, for he considered himself far more effective than any government agent. Besides, this was a job Deguere could stretch over many months, with Montrose funneling him money every few weeks. Caine's reputation as a hard catch made it all that much easier to extend the job for the highest cash value.

The case was proving to be more interesting and faceted than he would ever have thought. Deguere scanned his notebook, refreshing himself again on what he had learned these several months.

Through his own work and the help of investigative associates in Chicago, New York, and Washington, Deguere had pieced together a detailed working biography of Caine

and his associations. Through this process Deguere had long
known, for example, how Caine's brother had changed his
name to Brice James and married the daughter of famed
tycoon Garth Kensington. He had noted that since leaving
Montana, Caine had migrated toward Texas. That didn't
surprise Deguere, given the presence here not only of
Caine's brother, but also of his old wartime partner Drew
Strahan.

But it was another wartime associate whom Deguere
found particularly interesting. That was Neal Seahorn, believed dead by the public, but who loose-tongued government sources had said was not dead at all, and who was
deeply involved in a very covert Confederate-based criminal
conspiracy most commonly called the Alianza. The government sources told Deguere's investigators that Seahorn was
believed to be somewhere in Mexico's border country west of
the Rio Bravo, or Rio Grande, between El Paso and the Big
Bend region.

At first, the mysterious Alianza seemed mostly a curiosity to Deguere, but then something unexpected happened:
Caine's trail and that of Neal Seahorn and the Alianza began
to converge much more closely.

It first came clear in Wichita, Kansas, when Deguere
talked to residents of a boarding house in which Caine had
briefly lived under his alias of Robert Cole. Without revealing
the so-called Cole's true identity, Deguere found that Caine
had left Wichita after receiving a letter. A nosy fellow house
resident had seen a flash of the note, enough to detect that it
was calling its recipient to Serveto, Mexico, to meet a man
named Seahorn.

"Unusual name, 'Seahorn,'" the neighbor had said to
Deguere. "Just like the old war renegade the *federales* killed
a few years ago."

Deguere had said, yes, indeed, that is unusual, tipped
his hat, and left with a smile on his face and an impression
that a puzzle was coming together almost of its own accord.
He had just by luck discovered that Neal Seahorn was hiding
out in Serveto.

Deguere had put his horse in a boxcar and headed south

from Kansas, certain that in Texas he would easily pick up Caine's trail.

It didn't prove as easy as expected. Caine seemed to have vanished like a dust devil, and try as he would, Deguere could not fall back in his track. In near desperation he had gone to the Kensington ranch, figuring Caine had probably gone there to meet his brother and might be there yet.

Deguere found the ranch in turmoil, its personnel walking around with fear on their faces. He asked to see Brice James but was told he was gone. No, we don't know when he will return. No, you may not see Garth Kensington because he is ill. Please leave now, sir, and come again when the situation is better, and that may take a long time.

It was obvious something was amiss at the Kensington ranch, and Deguere wondered if it had to do with Caine. He made a few subtle inquiries about what had happened at the ranch but was unable to learn anything. At last he had mounted and headed toward Serveto, hoping to pick up Caine's path in that way.

Instead he spotted Brice James. Deguere studied the man through his spyglass and recognized him from an old photograph he possessed of the Caine family. When Brice dismounted to adjust his saddle, Deguere saw his limp and cinched the identification. Now this was intriguing: Why would Brice James be riding alone through this wilderness? And where was Simon Caine?

Deguere followed Brice James until he came to Drew Strahan's place. Brice stayed there only briefly, then quickly rode out toward the Mexican border. Deguere had almost followed him, then decided to turn back and interrogate Strahan. Deguere was glad he had, for otherwise he would not have learned about the kidnapping until it was too late to benefit him.

Deguere jotted more notes into his book. An amazing twist this was: Caine gone to meet Seahorn, apparently not knowing Seahorn had abducted his own nephew. Now Brice James was himself riding toward Serveto to try to rescue the boy . . . and in the background a criminal organization that smelled of big money—money Deguere wouldn't mind getting his hands into even as he continued his lucrative quest for Caine.

Deguere heard something that made him put away the notebook. Distant shots, echoing across the land . . .

Deguere looked across the desert. Dust was blowing in a kicking wind, and he could see nothing, no one. He heard what might have been another shot, but the wind shifted and carried the phantom sound away.

After a few more minutes of rest, Deguere resettled his derby on his head, mounted again, and began riding toward the Rio Bravo and the crossing that led to Serveto.

The first shot had spooked Brice's horse, which threw him to the dirt. The second blasted sand into his face, and the third clipped off a bit of his hair.

By the time the fourth came, Brice lay on his belly amid a pile of rocks, peering through the spears of a Spanish dagger plant, trying to pinpoint the spot from where the shots were erupting.

A fifth shot, an explosion of smoke. Brice fired a responding round from his Colt—but had no clear target.

A shadow moved across him. He rolled and saw a tall Anglo, wild-eyed and seemingly big as a grizzly, descending on him, knife drawn. Brice whipped up the pistol, firing it clumsily from stomach level, and then the Anglo was atop him, dead even as his breath hissed out. The knife stuck into the ground beside Brice's ear.

Trapped beneath the dead weight of the corpse, Brice panicked. His pistol lay across his stomach, pressing into him under the dead man's belly. Straining, Brice managed to pull it free just as another man, this one Mexican, appeared over the rim of boulders. Brice fired and the man fell back, crying out. Brice heard him writhe unseen on the other side of the rocks, then go silent.

Brice struggled out from beneath the dead man and rose to a crouched position. Nothing moved out across the undulating desert except the hypnotic waves of heat.

Something behind, a noise—

Brice spun just as a third bandido appeared. He wrenched

his bad leg beneath him and fell as he shot at him. The bandido laughed and aimed at Brice's face.

"Drop it, *compadre*."

Helplessly, Brice let his Colt fall. Two other men appeared almost magically, rising from behind rocks and cacti.

"We want money, *señor*."

"I have no money."

The Mexican cursed in Spanish. Brice saw he was about to shoot, and instinctively he ducked to the ground, awaiting the fatal blast.

Shots fired out as expected, but Brice was surprised to find he was not harmed. He looked up at the Mexican. The man had a strange look on his face. He softly grunted, lurched, and fell sideways. The other men shouted and scattered. Brice grabbed his pistol again.

The drylands came alive with activity.

Repeated shots, fired in a steady rhythm, boomed to Brice's left. To his right he heard more yells and screams from his surprised ambushers.

Then, as suddenly as it all had happened, there was silence. Brice lay still for another few seconds, catching his breath.

Someone trudged up to him. Brice saw a pair of booted feet. His eyes trailed up a pair of long, sturdy legs clad in canvas pants that were tucked into the boottops to keep scorpions out. He saw a gunbelt holding an 1860 model .44-caliber Colt Army pistol, well-kept despite its age. Across the crook of the man's arm lay Tandy Jones's rare and beloved Colt revolving rifle.

"Orion, I told you not to follow me," Brice said.

The handsome young black man grinned. "Yeah. Ain't you glad I didn't listen?"

"But how did you know where I was?"

"I didn't, exactly. But you said you were heading to Serveto, so I just did the same. Didn't expect to find you like this." He gestured toward the dead men. "Were they looking for your ransom money?"

"I don't think so. They asked for money, but they didn't

call it ransom. I think they jumped me just because I was alone."

"You're not as alone as you think. There's someone else trailing you, too."

"Who?"

"Don't know. I've found scraps of sign here and there— enough to make me sure."

Brice shook his head. The last thing he needed was somebody following him for nonexistent ransom.

After they had talked a bit more, Orion looked again at the bodies and asked, "Should we bury them?" The corpses lay sprawled within an area about twenty feet square.

"Nope," Brice said. "Let the buzzards have them. I wonder, is one of them Cato Blake?"

Orion shook his head. "If it was, we'd be dead now. Besides, I've seen Blake before. None of these is him."

Orion walked to one of the dead men, who stared up at the sky with his mouth open. A scorpion skittered across the man's chest, and flies were already buzzing and lighted around the staring blank eyes. Orion's expression was a bit peculiar, Brice noticed.

"First one you kill is always the hardest," Brice said. "I remember my first, during the war. I can still see the face."

Orion looked at Brice. "This ain't my first. I kilt my first back at the ranch after you left."

Brice looked amazed.

"Hosea Scruggs," Orion said.

"Hosea? For God's sake, why?"

"He went to Felipe drunk and laughing and saying it was him what helped the kidnappers get Keelan and kill my father. Felipe told me and I just went loco. I got out Pa's old Colt rifle here and went looking. I found him."

Brice was stunned. "Why would Hosea do such as that?"

"He was paid."

Orion scanned over the bodies of the dead ambushers again and shook his head. "But I'm nothing but a common outlaw now, Mr. Brice. I've kilt men."

"Just one traitor and one common bandit is all you've killed."

"Don't matter. I kilt them, and I'm colored, and that puts me at odds with the white law."

Brice knew Orion was right. No matter what the circumstances of his actions, many Anglos would gladly string him up without worrying over finer distinctions.

"You mind riding with a common outlaw, Mr. Brice?" Orion asked.

"You're no outlaw." Brice hesitated a moment, made a decision, then went on, "And even if you were, you wouldn't be the first I've been associated with. Close associated. Blood kin."

Orion looked confused, then his eyes widened. "You ain't kin to no Jesse James, are you ?"

Brice laughed. "No. But I have a brother you've heard of. He's one I've acted ashamed of a long time—but it's him I came looking for out here. If you're going to ride with me, you may as well know all the truth."

Brice told the full story: his brotherhood to Simon, his own change of name, Simon's recent return, everything. Orion listened, looking astounded, nodding occasionally as Brice went along.

Chapter 8

Brice and Orion forded the Rio Bravo. The water was up and the horses had to swim. Upon reaching the other side, they let them rest.

Brice knelt and idly scratched in the dirt with a stick. "How are we going to do this, Orion?" he asked despairingly. "We're two men against Lord only knows how many."

"That won't stop me," Orion said. "That was my Pa they kilt. What did you plan to do if you had found Simon Caine?" He chuckled. "I just can't get used to thinking of you as an outlaw's brother."

"I don't know what we would have done. I suppose I had hoped Simon would know what to do. He's good at these kinds of things." Suddenly he stopped, lifting a hand. "Did you hear that?"

"I did," Orion said. "Sounds like horses. A lot of them. Bandidos?"

"Could be. Let's find out."

They began a careful exploration, and several minutes later they hid their horses at the base of a rock formation that lay like a gigantic flat wedge against the land. They worked quietly up the long slope of it, and at the edge, where the formation cut off sharply into a bluff about twenty feet high, they gained a view of a drama being played out below.

A dozen riders were approaching a broad, shrub-filled depression about a hundred yards straight ahead. The riders pulled to a halt and dismounted hurriedly, like cavalrymen being ambushed. But it was clear that if any ambush was taking place here, the riders were the instigators, not the victims.

"What do you make of it?" Orion whispered.

"I'm not sure. They don't look like your usual bandidos. See the Mex in the fancy clothes? Dandier than any desert robber I've seen."

The gunmen below crept through the brush toward the basin. Brice noted an Appaloosa some distance beyond the depression. It was saddled, but riderless, and he knew none of the visible gunmen had been on it. It must be the mount of whoever was in the basin.

"Whoever's in that hole's not got a Chinaman's chance," Brice said.

One of the men below shouted, "Don't make us kill you, Caine! Seahorn wants you back alive!"

Brice exclaimed, "That's Simon they got down there!" He bolted up, but Orion pulled him back down.

"No, Mr. Brice. There's too many. You get killed and what happens to Keelan? Maybe your brother will surrender and they won't kill him."

"He doesn't surrender easy, Orion."

Suddenly the gunmen below leaped forward and fired down into the depression. The shots made popping sounds in the hot air.

Brice bowed his head, not wanting to look. "Too late," he said.

Fadden sat beside the fire, taking big swallows from a brown bottle of whiskey. Finally he rose, staggered slightly, and walked to the edge of the camp where Simon Caine was tied to a gnarled mesquite. Caine had a bandage around his calf, covering a bloody scrape wound left by a passing slug. It was the only wound he had received before being struck down in the basin by one of the gunmen who had leaped upon him from behind and struck his head with his rifle butt.

Fadden took another swallow, then squatted. He shoved the bottle forward toward Caine, who shook his head.

"Suit yourself, *compadre*," Fadden said. He turned the bottle up again; his throat moved as he swallowed. Then he corked the bottle and belched loudly and sourly from deep in his belly. "Bad stomach and bad whiskey don't mix," he said. "Hey, Caine, I thought we were going to have to kill you to get you out of that hole. You're one hellcat, you are. You ought to work for Seahorn. He could use you."

"I got no use for Seahorn," Caine said.

"You got use for *dinero*, don't you? Seahorn's got plenty of it. Connections, you know. Big crime organization of rich and crazy old Confederates. Lots of power, lots of money." Fadden laughed. "You take the power. I'll take the money." He uncorked the bottle and took another swallow and began talking again. "Now Seahorn, well, I got no use for him neither. I work for the money he pays, not for him." Fadden smiled drunkenly, leaning forward. He said in a too-loud whisper, "Someday I might just put a bullet through Seahorn's brainpan and see what kind of cash he has squirreled away in that room he hardly ever leaves." He winked, laughed, took another swig of whiskey, and stumbled away.

Caine closed his eyes and dozed lightly. He was exhausted from the hard run. Also angry at himself for allowing himself to be cornered. Such a thing wouldn't have happened a few years ago, he thought. Must be getting old and slow.

He opened his eyes a little later and saw Ramon Fernandez standing where Fadden had been. The handsome Mexican was smoking a thin *cigarro*. He smiled at Caine.

"Are you comfortable, Señor Caine?"

"Cut me loose, Fernandez. I'll ride out of here and you'll never see me again."

Fernandez took a drag and shook his head. "I'm sorry, *amigo*. I would gladly free you, but Neal Seahorn wants you back at Serveto."

"What does he need with me?"

"Oh, he could turn you in for reward, but I don't think that is his plan. You are being brought back for appearances, I think. You did what Seahorn will not allow, especially at a time his men are discontented: you defied him. He cannot afford to let his men see defiance go unanswered."

"His authority is slipping, then?"

"You are perceptive, *amigo*. Seahorn has made the mistake of surrounding himself with men who care nothing for loyalty and nothing for him. Money is their motivation, their true leader. Seahorn pays them well, but more and more they murmur about wealth they believe he hides from them. Alianza money. Soon Seahorn's men will rise against him and that will be the end of him and of Serveto."

Caine nodded. "I just heard the same from Fadden. It appears Neal wants me back to prove to his men he's still strong."

Ramon shook his head. "No, *amigo*. To prove it to himself. He is a coward in his heart, and ashamed of it. It is slowly driving him loco."

"Why do you stay?"

"Because at the moment I am content to be where I am." He smiled subtly. "And because I, too, think Seahorn has much wealth in his hands. Perhaps it is wise to play along for now, eh?"

Ramon flipped down the *cigarro*. "I will sleep now." He walked away.

The camp lay in a wide, flat expanse encircled by an uplifted rim of rock lined with brush. Atop that rim, unseen by Caine and all others in the camp, Brice lay with a knife in one hand, a pistol in the other. Orion was beside him.

"Wish me luck, and keep me covered," Brice whispered.

"Let me go with you," Orion said.

"No. Less dangerous with one. If they get me, Keelan's rescue is in your hands."

Brice slid through the brush and dropped lightly and silently to the edge of the basin. He crouched, put the knife in his teeth, and edged forward. He could make out the form of his brother limned against the fire.

Brice saw no movement in the camp and heard snores. He crept on, almost to Simon now...

Something moved. Brice dropped to his belly and lay still.

A Mexican walked up to Caine. "You make noise?" he asked Caine in Spanish. Caine did not respond. The Mexican drew back his foot as if to kick the prisoner, but then he looked into the brush and stopped. Brice pressed himself against the earth; he felt his heart pounding the ground.

The Mexican squinted almost directly toward Brice for a very long time. Brice became increasingly unnerved, but suddenly the Mexican shrugged, turned, and walked to the other side of the camp. Brice watched him until he was outside the sphere of light cast by the campfire.

Brice remained still a long time, then crabbed up behind Caine. He reached toward him, about to touch his shoulder...

Two things happened. Brice heard a scuffle and a thud behind him, where Orion was. At the same time, Fadden, who had been sleeping near the fire, awakened in a burst of coughing. He sat up, the firelight making his dark skin look like badly tarnished brass. Brice had no choice but to flatten again and stay frozen. Fadden sputtered and cursed beneath his breath, slid his bedroll farther from the fire, then lay down again. A few moments later Brice heard his grating snores resume.

Up again, and forward—Brice drew near to Simon, who now had noticed the stirring behind him and was trying to determine its origin without being obvious about it.

"Simon, it's me. I..."

Big hands grasped Brice's ankles and pull him backward. He dropped his knife. Brice fell on his face as he was dragged away and rolled over. He still grasped his pistol, but a booted foot came down hard on it and he could not lift it.

It was the big Mexican who had peered so suspiciously into the brush before. He had apparently left the camp on the far side and quietly walked the perimeter of it until he had found Brice. Brice feared for Orion.

The Mexican had a rock in his hand. He aimed it at Brice's head and came down with it. Brice shouted and rolled; the rock pounded the dirt beside his ear. The Mexican became unbalanced and lifted his weight enough to allow Brice to scramble to his feet. Brice fired but missed. At a dead run, Brice made for the brush-lined basin rim.

The Mexican drew his pistol and fired it. Brice felt the wind of the slug as it went past him. He hurried, dived for the brush, and found Orion just now pushing upright, rubbing the back of his head.

"Somebody hit me..."

"Come on!" Brice urged, pulling Orion to his feet.

Together they ran away from the camp, toward the place their horses were hidden. Voices and shouts assailed them from behind; they heard men coming after them. They ran harder.

Back in the camp, Caine struggled futilely with his bonds. He was surprised and confused. Whoever had come up and whispered behind him had sounded just like his brother. But how could that be?

Caine pulled again at his ropes but could not get free.

Seahorn walked across the plaza, past the well, toward the makeshift carcel of Serveto. He was uncomfortable away from his chambers; he would not have left them at all except the men he trusted least were still out searching for Caine.

A huge bonfire cast light across the hard-pounded dirt and made jumpy shadows beneath the arches of nearby doorways and portal columns. Somewhere in the darkness someone played a guitar and sang an old Mexican lament.

A sentinel seated by the doorway stood when Seahorn approached, but seeing who it was, he first looked surprised and then stepped aside.

Inside the dingy building lamps dimly lit the passageway. Seahorn walked down it, pausing at Keelan's door. He looked through the little barred window. Keelan lay sleeping. He counted back the days. Anytime now the boy's father should be here with the ransom. A quarter of a million dollars—the thought of that gave Seahorn a warm feeling beneath his skin.

He went farther down the passage. Another sentinel stood by a door there.

"The key," Seahorn said. The sentinel gave it to him.

Seahorn unlocked the door and entered.

Rosalita got up from her cot. Still wearing her dress, she was unkempt and tired-looking. She picked up her blanket and wrapped it around her shoulders.

"There are rats here," she said. "They run across me when I sleep. Let me go."

Seahorn scowled. "Why should I? You betrayed me. Caine was an important prisoner and you helped him escape."

"I am sorry. I was a fool."

"I don't dispute that. But sorrow isn't enough to earn your freedom."

"My husband died in your service. Does that earn me no privilege?"

"Your husband, my dear Rosalita, meant nothing." Seahorn's smile became different and frightening. "I hired him for one reason. You. You do know you are a beautiful woman, do you not, Rosalita?"

He advanced. She backed away.

"I would rather die," she said.

"I can easily arrange that," Seahorn responded. "But there is no need for it. Come, Rosalita. I have been thinking of you. Be cooperative and you will go free."

"I hate you!" she spat.

Seahorn lunged at her, grasping at her dress. Screaming, she kicked his shin, then slapped him. Her fingernails raked bloody furrows down his cheek.

Seahorn swore, backed off, and touched his hand to his face. He looked at the blood on his fingers.

"You just signed your own death warrant, sow!" he shouted at her. He spun and left the filthy chamber, slamming the door shut. He pushed past the sentinels and exited onto the plaza. When he was gone, the sentinels looked at each other and laughed, for they had heard everything, and one had watched through the window.

In his room down the passageway, Keelan wrapped his blanket into a tight roll and buried his head beneath it. He had been awakened by the turmoil, and now a woman was crying in the next room and he did not want to hear it.

Chapter 9

Seahorn dined alone at his table. Before him stood some of his men and Simon Caine. Caine was grimed and somewhat bloody.

"How hard did he resist?" Seahorn asked.

Fadden, slouching as usual, his lower lip drooping beneath his cigarette, shrugged with one shoulder. "Not hard enough," he said. "But I thought we'd have to kill him, I did."

Seahorn wiped his lips, stood, and approached Caine. He looked into his face and gave him a smug, tight-lipped smile. "You should have joined me to begin with," he said. "And you certainly shouldn't have tried to escape me."

Caine's throat felt like the floor of the Chihuahuan Desert. "You're loco," he said.

"I am a leader. A leader must be followed."

"You're not my leader."

"Then I'll be your captor."

"What do you want done with him?" Fadden asked.

"I haven't decided. Perhaps we will gather a reward for him. Perhaps we will just keep him locked up for a long, long time. I could have you killed, perhaps—but we are old friends, are we not, Simon?" Seahorn waved his hand. "Take him away. Lock him up and make sure he is well guarded."

"The storeroom again?"

"No. This time the carcel."

Ramon Fernandez had been standing to the rear, but now he stepped forward. "Neal, there's something you should know. Two men, an Anglo and a black man, tried to free Caine last night. We chased them, but they escaped us."

Seahorn's face darkened. "Did Caine know them?"

"He says he didn't. But he did not see their faces."

"Who were they, Simon?" Seahorn demanded.

"Lee and Grant."

Seahorn cursed. He drew a pistol from beneath his coat and whipped it down on Caine's head. Caine fell unconscious. "Take him away," Seahorn ordered. "Get him out of my sight."

Seahorn mulled it all as Caine was carried across the broad Serveto plaza. Who could have been trying to free Simon Caine, especially from such a large armed band?

The sun was distended and red like an overripe strawberry as it edged down toward the western mountains. The evening was cloudy and windy. Seahorn poured himself a shot of whiskey. Standing at the window, he looked across the enclosure, watching the movement of people below. He watched Fadden and two others carrying Caine into the carcel, drawing much attention from others. Ramon, however, was walking across the other side of the plaza toward the cantina, having taken his leave from Fadden as quickly as possible. Seahorn could not blame him; Fadden was a repulsive man, and not inspiring of trust. Trust was becoming a rare commodity to Seahorn as well; he knew even Ramon was not as loyal as he acted.

Cattle lowed somewhere to the east, and in some alleyway two tomcats squared off in a loud and violent battle. Probably for the affections of some female—and with that Seahorn was reminded of Rosalita Contero's spurning. The thought was welcome as a swallow of gall.

Seahorn drained off his glass and forced his thoughts onto another track. He looked over the old mission wall toward the notch of Puerta de Serveto. Soon, if all went well, the ransom for the Kensington boy should arrive through that rock gateway.

Seahorn thought about that quarter of a million dollars, and again about leaving the Alianza. He was tired of its control, but mostly he was scared. He could feel the Alianza breathing upon him, bearing down, knowing of his embezzlements and preparing some retribution.

Maybe he should leave tonight. But if he did, he would have none of that quarter million dollars in ransom.

Unless—the thought burst upon him—he simply took the boy with him. Kidnapped him anew, in effect, and snatched him right out from beneath the nose of the Alianza. He could take the boy deep into Mexico, find some place where the Alianza couldn't reach them, and when the time was right, demand a new and bigger ransom from Kensington. This ransom he would share with no one except Old Pablo. He would find his old mentor and take him somewhere deep into South America, and there they could live splendidly the rest of their days.

He was becoming excited now. He put down his glass and turned to a heavy door leading into a small hall just off his chamber. Dark and dusty, this passage was used by no one but himself. He lit a match and walked by its light to the end, where he fitted a key into a heavy lock and opened another door, this one reinforced with iron bands.

A squat, fat safe stood before him. He lit a candle in a wall holder and knelt, turning the combination dial. He opened the safe with a creak.

The candlelight revealed stacks of money, wages to be paid by him for the Alianza and that he had embezzled. He picked up some of the bills and moved them between his fingers.

The light around him changed. He turned, standing, quickly putting the bills back into the safe. He closed the safe door with his foot, touched his hand to his pistol butt.

"*Salud*, Neal."

"Ramon, I might have killed you."

Ramon's eyes flickered around the little room. This was the first time he had been here. "You spend much time here, eh, Neal?"

"It's no concern of yours."

"Of course not. Forgive me. But come out, then. I have something to say to you."

They left the chamber and Seahorn closed the door. In

Ramon's eyes was a look of concern, maybe anger, though hidden beneath his eternally calm veneer.

"What is wrong?" Seahorn asked.

"I was told you locked up Rosalita Contero."

"I had no choice. She helped Simon Caine escape."

"I want her."

A long silence followed. Peculiar emotions raged through Seahorn. He forced a smile. "I believe you care for her, Ramon."

"Call it what you want. I want her freed."

Seahorn paced in silence for a few moments, looking at the tiled floor. Though he hid it well, jealousy burned inside him. Ramon's handsome face, his calm, dignified manner—these things would probably win the affections Rosalita had denied Seahorn, and Seahorn knew it. But he merely nodded to Brice.

"Very well. She is your care. But remember, Ramon: She betrayed me. She may betray you as well."

Seahorn went to a desk, pushed back the roll top, and wrote a directive on a piece of paper. He signed it with his unmistakable flourished signature and handed it to Ramon, who took the paper wordlessly and turned away.

"How long have you had your eye on her, Ramon?"

"Had Juan Contero not been killed in the kidnapping, I would have killed him upon his return. Quietly, secretly. Perhaps an accident."

"I will tell you something before she does," Seahorn said. "I went to her last night. She is a beautiful woman. I could not resist."

Ramon glared threateningly. "Did you . . ."

"No."

Ramon exhaled. "That is good, because if you had, I would have killed you, *amigo*."

Seahorn looked coldly at him. He pulled a cigarette from a wooden case and lit it as Ramon walked out, paper in hand.

Seahorn smoked and thought. This was a night for decisions, and he made one.

He went to the window and called to a man passing below: "Bring me Fadden at once."

He finished his cigarette and waited.

Fifteen minutes later, J. W. Fadden sat slouched in one of Seahorn's overstuffed chairs, picking at a thumbnail and looking, as always, devoid of concern about anything at all. But that was a contrived appearance; he was very interested in what Seahorn had just ordered him to do.

"When?" he asked.

"As quickly as is feasible. Do not fail. I can no longer trust him, and she has betrayed me . . . betrayed the Alianza already. There will, of course, be much good money in it for you."

"Mighty fine." Fadden stood, stretching like a rumpled old tomcat. "I won't let you down," he said. He walked to the door and left.

For seemingly endless hours, Brice and Orion had been picking their way along through rocky hills that wind and desert rains had carved into a series of piled terraces that were difficult to maneuver about. The horses had a hard time of it here, and they stopped frequently to let them rest. Orion used his hat to water them out of a water bag carried on one of the packhorses. The red sun declined and night spread across the dry barrens.

"Can't go much farther tonight, Mr. Brice," Orion said.

But Brice was eager. "Moonlight's bright, and its cool. Let's go as far as we can."

He was thinking much of Keelan tonight, but also of Simon. He wondered what had become of his brother. Probably he was dead now. Brice regretted the years of estrangement from his brother. The old arguments and divisions seemed unimportant now.

At least, he thought, Simon died on the right side. He had apparently not cooperated with Seahorn. Based on what he had been told by Strahan and what he had seen and heard on his own, it was easy for Brice to piece together what must have happened. Simon had gone to Serveto, somehow angered Seahorn, and then escaped. Seahorn had sent the riders after him, and Simon had been recaptured and taken back. Probably he had been executed.

But maybe not. *If you're alive, Simon, and if I can, I'll try to get you out, too,* Brice inwardly vowed.

"Listen!" Orion whispered. "Somebody following us."

They quickly cut right into a small canyon, and there they waited. No sound stirred except that of the wind through the rock maze.

"I swear I heard something back there," Orion said.

"Let's make camp here," Brice suggested. "We'll post watch for a time and see what turns up."

Orion nodded. Somewhere out there a coyote howled.

Chapter 10

Hours passed, and Orion and Brice heard and saw nothing to indicate there was anyone on their trail. Eventually both exhausted men nodded and fell asleep.

Morning light and the smell of coffee awakened Brice. He rolled over, groaning, and rubbed his head as he yawned himself back to consciousness. The coffee scent was enticing, but he was surprised Orion had risked building a fire to brew it.

He opened his eyes. Orion was only now stirring awake. After a few groggy moments of realization, Brice leaped up.

A stranger with a tin coffee cup in his hand sat on a rock a few yards away from a small mesquite fire. He lifted the cup as if in toast to Brice.

"Good morning," the stranger said. He was a small-framed but solid man in fancy riding clothes, and he had a fine auburn beard parted at the chin. His derby sat on his knee.

"Who are you?" Brice demanded, looking around for his pistol.

Morrison Deguere smiled and said, "My name is Hugh Talbot." From his manner one would surmise there was nothing unusual about his sudden appearance and his building of the fire.

"What are you doing in our camp?" queried Orion, who now had come around and ascertained the circumstances. Orion had done better than Brice; the young black man already had his revolving Colt rifle up and trained on Deguere.

"I'm here to help you, gentlemen," he said. "Let me congratulate you on leaving a rather difficult trail. For a time I thought I would not find you."

"You know us?" Brice asked.

"You are Brice James, and prior to that you were James Brice Caine. You are the son-in-law of Garth Kensington, the brother of Simon Caine, and you are on your way to Serveto to attempt to reclaim your kidnapped son. As for you, young man," he said to Orion, "you are a surprise. I confess I don't know you nor did I expect to find any but Mr. James here in this camp. Nevertheless, accept my hellos."

"You'll be saying hello to Jesus if you twitch," Orion said.

"Believe me, I will remain still. I will do you no harm. In fact, I feel sure I can do you some good."

"Who are you—besides your name?" Brice asked.

"I am an agent of the United States Department of the Treasury's Secret Service."

"Secret Service . . ." Brice developed a sudden suspicion. "You're after my brother."

"Simon Caine? Heavens, no." Deguere laughed. "I'm seeking much bigger game than he. I'm after the Alianza. Do you know what that is?"

"I know Neal Seahorn's in it, and that he's got my boy."

"Precisely. The Alianza is also a growing source of counterfeit currency, and of threats against the safety of certain federal officials and American citizens. The Treasury Department is quite concerned."

"So they send out one man? You're a liar."

"They sent out five of us as an investigative team. Two were killed, two were wooed into the Alianza. But I have no plan to attempt a single-handed overthrow of such a massive crime system. I am a fact-gatherer, that is all. Though I admit the kidnapping of your son has persuaded me to expand my role somewhat. I want to help you get him out—and in the process get inside the walls of Serveto. There is where I can really learn what the Alianza is about, and what Seahorn's role in it is.

"Seahorn is wanted very badly by the federal government at the moment, as you might imagine. We believe he

might be persuaded, by threat or leniency, to provide important evidence against the Alianza."

Brice shook his head. "Why should we trust you? Show
some proof of your identity."

Deguere chuckled. "A man does not enter the territory
of Mexican bandidos and antigovernment criminal conspira-
tors and carry such identification. Such a man would find
himself quickly dead."

"So all we have is your word as to who you are?"

"Precisely."

"How did you know me? And how did you know about
Simon—and the kidnapping?"

"It shouldn't surprise you that a Secret Service agent
would know about Simon Caine and his kin, should it? You
have hidden your kinship to him well, Mr. James, but the
federal government knows of it. It is our job to know such
things. Consider the Alianza, for instance. What the Alianza
does I find out about one way or another, sooner or later. But
in your case my knowledge isn't as mysterious as it sounds.
Unfortunately, word of the kidnapping of your son has spread.
You need all the assistance you can get, Mr. James."

Orion still held the Colt rifle aloft. "He's lying, Mr.
Brice. I guarantee you nobody at the ranch has breathed a
word about the kidnapping. Want me to kill him?"

"No. Put the rifle down, Orion."

"But he—"

"Put it down."

Reluctantly, Orion obeyed.

"We've already been attacked by one small group," Brice
said. "Orion is an old friend who came along at the right time
to keep me from being murdered. The Alianza killed Orion's
father—he has reason to hate it just like I do. Now, how do
you propose to help me?"

"If nothing else, I will strengthen your number by one.
Against bandidos and mercenaries that counts for little, I
know, but little is better than nothing. Besides, as I said, I
need to get inside Serveto. Working together, perhaps we can
achieve that. I don't know how I could do it alone."

"Let me shoot him, Mr. Brice," Orion urged again.

Brice shook his head. "No. Mr. Talbot, I may be a fool, but I'll trust you, partly because I can at least keep my eye on you if you're close by. And you're right: I need what help I can get. I came looking for Simon's, but that didn't work out."

Deguere said, "It's my belief that Simon Caine was headed for Serveto. Is he there?"

Brice was impressed that the false Talbot knew as much as he did. He instinctively began to trust him just a bit more, telling him briefly about Simon's apparent escape and recapture.

Deguere sipped his coffee. "Seahorn may indeed kill him," he said. "If so, he will have achieved something scores of others have failed to do. But if I were a betting man, I'd put my money on Caine. He's a hard man to kill."

He tossed the coffee on the little fire, extinguishing it. "Have some coffee while it's still hot, gentlemen," he said. "It's growing too light to keep a fire burning. Then let us move on. In following you yesterday I found evidence of horsemen about. Bandidos, probably. By the way, do you actually have the ransom with you?"

"No," Brice said. "If I'm going to trust you, I may as well tell you. The Kensington empire is bankrupt."

Deguere clicked his tongue. "A shame. You can count on my silence. We certainly wouldn't want Neal Seahorn to hear that the well from which he expects to draw his latest fortune has run dry."

"No, we wouldn't." Brice turned to Orion. "Let's move on."

"I still think you ought to let me shoot him," Orion said.

The sentinel who brought food to Caine's cell looked inside, smirked, and said, "Smell the sweet perfume of this cell, Caine? It was home to a beautiful woman. Believe me, you are a far uglier sight than the widow Rosalita Contero, *amigo*."

Caine started. "Rosalita Contero was a prisoner?"

"Do not ask about her, *amigo*. Ramon Fernandez, he may become jealous and . . ." The Mexican put his finger across his neck in the universal throat-cutting gesture.

Caine was dismayed. If Rosalita was a prisoner, it could

only mean her help to him had been detected and she had been punished for it.

"Where is she now?" he asked.

"Probably in Ramon's bed," the man said. "He came and took her away with him. He had a paper from Seahorn that said he could do so. You were unconscious when he came to take her."

The sentinel left, and Caine sat down on the chain-hung bunk. He wondered if Rosalita was all right and regretted that he had been the cause of her trouble. Perhaps Ramon would take care of her, protect her—but Caine didn't really trust Ramon any more than he did Seahorn.

Caine believed that unless he came up with some plan of escape, Seahorn would eventually have him killed for lack of any other good options. Caine was a threat to both Seahorn and the Alianza now, so even if Seahorn didn't really want him dead, in the end it would probably come to that anyway. Unless . . .

What? Caine searched his options and found only two. The first: He could tell Seahorn he had changed his mind and was ready to join with him—but Seahorn would be unlikely to believe that. Which left only the second option—escape once more.

But this time it would be much more difficult. Maybe impossible.

Caine ate and then lay down. He needed to gather his strength as he thought out a plan. But he was tired and after a few minutes fell asleep.

The sound of someone crying awakened him. It was deep night. He pushed up, for a moment not remembering where he was.

"Hello?" he said lowly.

The crying continued. It sounded like a child, probably a boy. He remembered then what he had overheard before his escape—a boy kidnapped.

Caine rose. He cupped his hands on the wall and spoke into them, concentrating his voice so it would pass through the stone.

"Son—you all right?"

The crying stopped. He heard sniffles. "I'm all right," a youngster's voice returned. "I'm just scared."

Caine could barely hear the boy and told him so.

"There's a hole through the wall down at the floor," the boy said. "The rats go in and out through it. If we get down there, we can talk through it."

Caine did that. As he did, he had the mental experience that talking to children usually brought him: a flash of perfectly clear memory of his own son, Marcus—his face, his voice, his eyes. All now forever gone.

The hole was small but sufficient to allow Caine to see a little into the next room. He had to force himself to ignore the vermin droppings in which he had to lay in order to peer through the opening. Suddenly he saw the boy's eye looking back at him, no more than a foot away. Caine could see only that eye, yet he could tell when the boy smiled. He smiled back.

"Be brave, young fellow," Caine said. "I'm planning to get us out of here." And so he was; the moment he had heard the boy cry, he had, without conscious thought, expanded his hope of escape to include escape for the boy, too. If Caine thought about it, which he did not, he would have realized that the escape of the boy was now in fact becoming more important to him than his own.

"I am brave," the boy said. "My pa taught me to be. But in here it's hard sometimes."

"I know," Caine said. "It looks to me like we're two jackrabbits caught in the same snare."

"Are you kidnapped, too?" the boy asked.

"No. I just happened to get on the wrong side of somebody important here."

"What's your name?"

"Simon."

"Simon who?"

"Simon's good enough." Caine was getting an almost eerie feeling: something about the boy was uncannily familiar. Caine searched his mind to determine where he might have seen him.

"My name is Keelan. I'm kidnapped. But my pa and

grandpa will pay to get me out. Then they'll have the bad men arrested and the Texas Rangers will hang them all."

"So they might, Keelan. Who's your folks?"

"My grandpa is Garth Kensington. My pa is Brice James."

There was no sound from the other side for a long time. The boy looked through the hole again; no one was looking back.

"Mister? Are you there? Mister?"

The eye returned, looking back into Keelan's.

"Mister? You all right?"

"I'm all right, son. And you're going to be all right, too. I promise."

Chapter 11

Ramon Fernandez strode back toward his quarters with two long loaves beneath his arm. It was not yet dawn, but he was hungry and stirred the baker early from his own bed and bought the loaves for his breakfast, and Rosalita's.

Ramon lived in an upper-level room in the building that once housed the Serveto Mission nuns' quarters. He had never particularly liked the drab place, but now that Rosalita was with him it seemed much brighter and inviting—even if so far Rosalita had spurned his affection, treating him with an uncomfortable combination of gratitude for his rescuing her from the carcel and seeming disgust at his touch. Ramon didn't really mind—so far. She was an interesting challenge. He had cast his eye on Rosalita a long time ago, well before the death of her husband.

Ramon climbed the stairs and mounted the balcony, but at the full-length window he paused, some instinct warning him. He touched the latch and cautiously pushed the window open.

"Rosalita?"

He dropped the loaves and drew his pistol. "Rosalita?"

She was not inside the main room. He slipped to the bedroom and saw her there, her face twisted in fear. J. W. Fadden held her from behind. His pistol was jammed against her temple.

Fadden's drooping lip curled into his typical sneer of a smile. "Hello, Ramon."

"Let her go."

"No can do. Got me a job, you see. Got to take care of a big Mex rat that's been nosing around Seahorn's grain pile too long. He wants rid of it."

Ramon took a long breath. He seemed to grow taller. "Seahorn sent you?"

"Surely did. But don't worry—I ain't inclined to do what he said to do."

"What?"

"I aim to let you do it yourself."

"No!" Rosalita cried. "Run, Ramon!" *Ironic*, Ramon thought, *at a time like this, she seems to care something about me*.

Fadden laughed. He squeezed Rosalita and cut off her breath. "Ramon won't run, pretty lady. He don't run from nothing," he said. "He's a brave man, you see. Brave enough to plug his own brain rather than see you lose yours all over these walls."

Ramon's finger moved microscopically on the trigger of his long pistol.

"Put that pistol to your noggin, Ramon."

Slowly Ramon's pistol went up. Rosalita began to cry.

"That's good, Ramon. That's right. Put it to your head . . . no—even better, in your mouth. That way you can't miss."

Ramon, his eyes boring into Fadden's, obeyed. Rosalita was near collapse; she hung in Fadden's grip.

"*Adios*, Ramon," Fadden said. "Do it."

"No!" Rosalita cried. "*Madre de Dios!*"

The sound of the shot echoed across the plaza of Serveto, awakening sleepers. Neal Seahorn was among them. He leaped from his bed, raced to the window, and flung it open. Below, people emerged into the plaza. Seahorn heard a woman scream, then another shot.

"Where?" Seahorn shouted at a man below.

"In Ramon's rooms," he said.

Seahorn looked across to the old nun's quarters. He smiled to himself as he turned.

But motion at Ramon's window suddenly caught the corner of his eye. The window swung open and someone emerged. Seahorn quailed. It was Ramon, and he was carrying the body of J. W. Fadden. Blood dripped from a hole in the forehead of the corpse.

The people in the plaza sent up sounds of surprise. Several laughed. Ramon walked down the stairs, carrying the body as if it weighed nothing, and strode across the plaza with it. Ramon looked up at Seahorn as he approached. He went out of sight, then Seahorn heard him coming up the stairway. With dread Seahorn went to his door and opened it.

Ramon came down the hall. Fadden's draining body was gruesome and pale.

Ramon dumped the corpse at Seahorn's feet. "Yours, *compadre?*" He wheeled and walked away.

It took Ramon a long time to comfort Rosalita. The bullet he had fired into the head of Fadden had passed within two inches of her own. Fadden's blood had splattered her, and even though Ramon had scrubbed it from her until her skin was coppery red, she still talked of it and wiped at her face.

At last she calmed as he held her.

"I want to leave this place," she said, her voice quaking.

"We will leave, soon, very soon. I will take you away."

"No. I want to go alone."

Ramon put his hands on her shoulders and pushed her back to look into her eyes. "Even now you will not have me?" he said. "Do you not realize he would have killed you had I not shot him?"

"I realize. But if I stay here, and if I stay with you, there will always be more of such things. I want only to live a quiet and peaceful life."

"Then live it with me. We will go away. I will learn to live differently."

"As what? A farmer? A merchant? You would have no patience with such things. Men such as you cannot change, Ramon. I lived too many years with one to believe differently."

"So you are rejecting me?"

"I am asking you to let me go. And another thing—to help me free Simon Caine again. I saw them bring him back to the carcel before you came for me. He looked almost dead."

Ramon's expression slowly hardened. Anger welled up. "So it is Caine who interests you," he said. He shoved her to the floor. He drew his pistol and thumbed back the hammer. "I ought to..."

Rosalita closed her eyes, fully expecting to die. But Ramon restrained himself. He lowered the hammer and holstered the pistol, then reached down and roughly pulled her up.

"Come, Rosalita. If it is Caine you want, you can have him. And the rats of the carcel."

"Let me go!" she shouted, trying to tug away.

Ramon smiled. "No. No. I was loco to free you. Let Seahorn and Caine have you. I don't want you."

He dragged her out and down the stairs. She screamed and fought, drawing stares and laughter from those in the plaza. Ramon ignored them all as he carried the writhing woman across the courtyard toward the makeshift carcel.

Neal Seahorn heard the commotion and walked out onto his balcony. He watched Ramon disappear around the carcel toward the door on the far side. Surmising that Rosalita was being reincarcerated, Seahorn smiled. She must have rejected Ramon, too. But his smile quickly faded, for he was worried.

Fadden had failed to kill Ramon, and Ramon obviously knew that Seahorn had been the one who was behind the attempt. Ramon would not let that pass.

Seahorn made up his mind: It was time to go.

The first slug came from above and almost took off Deguere's head. He dropped from his horse and scrambled to the rocks beside the narrow trail. He drew his pistol but wished he had been able to unboot his saddle carbine.

The packhorse spooked and tugged at its ties, broke free, and ran back down the trail. Orion Jones dropped out of his saddle, managing to take the burnished revolving Colt rifle with him. Brice reacted more slowly. A second shot winged down from the high rocks and almost struck his mount before he threw himself out of the saddle and landed roughly on the rocky trail. He popped up, drew out his own long arm, and ran for the trailside boulders.

"Where?" Brice shouted across to Deguere and Orion.

Orion answered by lifting the revolving Colt and firing upward, above Brice's head. Someone above cursed in Spanish and scrambled back.

More bandidos.

Now Brice saw movement above the other side of the narrow pass. "Look out!" he yelled. A huge boulder, dislodged by someone above, rolled down toward Orion and Deguere. They threw themselves to either side just in time to avoid being crushed, but the tail of Orion's duster was caught beneath the stone.

A bandido whooped like an Indian and appeared briefly where the boulder had been. He fired down, slugs spanging around Orion, who could not twist around sufficiently to retaliate. But Brice and Deguere fired simultaneously. Neither hit the bandido, but their shots forced the man to draw back behind the rocks above.

Orion was tugging at his duster tail, then he gave it up and began slipping out of the long trail coat. The move left him momentarily but helplessly bound up—and precisely then two horsemen pounded up the trail from behind, riding straight toward him.

Deguere stood, leveled his pistol, and fired. One of the riders pitched out of the saddle, then rose and ran for cover, gripping a bleeding arm. His riderless horse sped on by, kicking up dust and gravel. The second rider cursed and levered a carbine. Brice fired at him, missed, and Deguere lifted his pistol a second time. But a second boulder, much smaller, came tumbling from above and struck his shoulder, felling him roughly. He dropped his pistol as a miniature follow-up avalanche of gravel and fist-sized stones descended upon him, virtually burying him. Above, a jubilant bandido cheered at his success.

The bandido on the horse fired at Orion but missed. Brice was about to shoot at the man again when something struck the chamber of his rifle just above the trigger. A slug, fired from above and intended for his head, had missed and destoyed his gun instead. Brice tossed down the weapon and drew his pistol. But now two more riders came up the trail to join the one already there, and another horseman appeared from behind Brice. This one was a tall Anglo with deeply tanned skin and hair the color of the dust that now swirled through the little rocky pass.

The Anglo leveled a Smith & Wesson on Brice. "Drop it, friend. Now."

Brice obeyed. "You too, darky!" the man shouted at Orion. Orion's face twisted in a snarl of frustration as he complied.

Deguere dug himself out from under the pile of dirt and rock. He spat out dirt, glared angrily at the Anglo bandido leader, and began picking grit from his beard.

"Money," the Anglo said.

"We got no money," Brice returned. "That's the God's truth."

The Anglo fired a shot that almost pierced the toe of Brice's boot.

"Kill me and it won't help you," Brice said. "We don't have any money."

The bandidos were gathering around their leader, leaving their various ambush perches and mounts. The wounded one who had run away came back, right hand around left arm, blood running through fingers. In Spanish he urged the Anglo to kill them all.

"Shut up," the Anglo said. "I kill them after I find where the money is."

"You seem to have a problem with either your hearing or your comprehension, my friend," Deguere said.

"The Apaches have been known to pluck out white men's beards a hair at a time," the Anglo responded. "It's a skill I've learned from the best of them."

Deguere arrogantly lifted his brows. Even in the midst of this crisis, Brice almost laughed; this man had looked uppity even while sprawled on his rump.

"I know you," Orion said to the Anglo. "You're Cato Blake."

"Ah!" Deguere said. "Comanchero turned Mexican highwayman. A fitting step up for such an infamous gentleman."

The Anglo started to say something to Orion, but he got no further than opening his mouth. In silence he regarded the young black man, looking at him as if he recognized him. Suddenly he wheeled and looked at Brice just as closely. He tucked his Smith & Wesson back into the crossdraw rig he wore.

"*Amigos,* you got my apology," he said. "I didn't recognize you. You'll suffer no harm from Cato Blake."

Chapter 12

The pronouncement left Brice and Deguere confused and casting glances at each other.

"You're married to Garth Kensington's daughter, if I ain't mistaken," Cato Blake said to Brice. "I seen you one time—though you didn't see me."

"I don't understand," Brice admitted.

"Old man Kensington was good to me once when I was down and out," the outlaw said. "It was maybe six years ago, and I was on the run from some rangers. I'd stole a few sheep from an old Irishman about Presidio. Your pappy-in-law hid me out, give me some food, steered them rangers the wrong way. Said he liked the look of my face. I never forgot that. No, sir."

"But Garth always said..." Brice trailed off. He had started to comment on his father-in-law's apparent hatred of the infamous desert bandit Cato Blake, but he realized such might be dangerously imprudent at the moment. Thinking about it, though, it made more sense. Six years ago Blake was not the widely known criminal he was today, and it was just like Garth Kensington to take pity on some dusty loser on the run.

Deguere stood, dusting himself off. "Well, it's good it was sheep you stole. Had it been cattle, Kensington would have strung you up."

Cato looked at Deguere with a threatening expression. Brice stepped up quickly and thrust out his hand, hoping to avert trouble. Cato looked like the kind of man who might shoot an irritating stranger the way a man swats a bothersome fly.

"My name's Brice James. I'm not happy to have been shot at, but I appreciate you not killing me."

"Wouldn't have jumped you if I'd known you. The fact is, we were waiting for a group what's supposed to be hauling guns, dynamite, and whiskey into Serveto when you come along. One of the men got trigger-happy."

"Dynamite, you said?" Deguere's face had lost its smug expression. He now looked keenly interested.

"Yep. I don't know exactly what's going on in Serveto, but for the last month they've hauled in guns, freight, liquor. Even one kidnapped boy, so I hear."

"The boy—is he all right?" Brice asked eagerly.

Cato looked like a slow-thinking fellow, but the appearance was deceptive. He cocked his head and looked piercingly at Brice. "He wouldn't be your boy, would he?"

Brice nodded.

"Don't know whether he's all right or not. I didn't see him myself. Rico did, though." He waved toward the bandido with the bleeding arm, who glared back with his teeth gritted.

"These dynamite couriers—when will they be through?" Deguere asked.

Cato asked Brice, "Who is this jackass?"

Brice said, "A friend. He's going to help me get my boy back."

"Out of Serveto? You know what you're getting into?"

Deguere said, "When a small force takes on a large fortified one, a little equalization helps. That's why I asked about the dynamite."

Cato frowned. "I figure to keep that for myself. I don't recall making you any offers."

"It's your chance to repay your debt to Garth Kensington," Deguere urged. "You take the whiskey, the guns—just let us have some of the dynamite."

Cato said, "My debt to Garth Kensington was repaid the moment I let you boys keep breathing."

Orion, who up until now had been standing to the rear in silence, stepped up and joined Brice. He looked at Cato. "I remember you, mister," he said. "You hid out behind the grain bin for a day or so. I brung you your food."

"I remember, boy. I'm obliged to you."

"What about the dynamite?" Deguere said.

"Shut up," Brice cut in. He could tell the bandit disliked Deguere, whose pushiness might make his mercy wear thin. Brice turned to Cato. "Mr. Blake, as far as I'm concerned, you owe none of us a thing. But I do ask you this: For the sake of my boy, we could use at least a few sticks of that dynamite. I don't know how we'll use it or whether it will help, but it just might."

Rico of the bleeding arm began chattering angrily in a mixture of Spanish and English, protesting Brice's request. Cato listened to him until he was finished.

The outlaw sat down on a rock and put his elbow to his knee. Fingering his chin, he thought. The others watched silently as the wind whistled through the rock pass and the strayed horses began meandering back in to their owners.

Finally Cato stood. "All right," he said. "There'll be some dynamite for you. But you got to help me get it. After all, I didn't kill you, and you did wing Rico in his gun arm."

The way he said it made it sound as if not having murdered them before was an act of great magnanimity.

Brice felt a burst of the first authentic hope he had known since starting on this impossible venture.

With dynamite they might just be able to fight their way out of Serveto, if it came to that. They just might be able to rescue Keelan after all. Maybe even Simon, if he was still alive.

"You got a deal," Brice said. He extended his hand, and Cato shook it. The bandit's palm felt like the underside of an old boot worn out by sharp gravel.

"I'm just glad I was able to arrange this," Deguere said.

Caine sadly watched Rosalita Contero crying in the corner. The guards had brought her in shortly before and cast her roughly to the floor. They had lingered long enough to jest lewdly about the carnal opportunity they had just provided Caine, then they slammed the door shut. Rosalita had crawled to the corner and cried, and there she remained.

"I won't hurt you, Rosalita. You know that," Caine said.

He had said it to her several times before, but she had not responded.

But now she turned her reddened eyes on Caine. "I know," she said. "But Seahorn will. He has already tried to kill Ramon—I think because of me."

"What happened?"

She told him about the attack and resultant death of J. W. Fadden.

"Interesting," Caine said. "The powers that be in Serveto fighting among themselves. What will Ramon do now that he knows Seahorn wants him dead?"

"I think he will kill him. But first he wants to steal his money."

Caine said, "Listen to me. There's a boy in the next room, and I aim to get him out of here. You, too. You helped me out once, I'll help you out now."

Rosalita wiped her face. "How?"

"I haven't fully figured that yet," Caine said. "Seems to me there's only a couple of things that would persuade our guards to let us slip: the threat of death, or the promise of reward."

"But we have no weapons, and no money," Rosalita said.

"No money, you're right. But there's always a weapon."

Rosalita smiled and nodded. "Sometimes a woman can be the best weapon, no?"

Caine smiled, too. "That's a fact."

Despite the pact between Brice and himself, Cato insisted on thoroughly searching his new partners. He found a hip flask of good whiskey on Deguere and immediately claimed it as his own. He began drinking it as the band hid among the boulders above the rocky pass, and his tongue loosened and gave forth his personal history.

"I was borned in Arkansas, but my ma, she died a few days after and I don't remember her. Pa wasn't no good and I wasn't either. We come across Texas, mostly running from the law, and crossed the Pecos. Apache trouble, Comanches, other outlaws, nothing stopped us. Pa up and died on me one night. Got drunk and choked to death on a piece of melon rind. I come across the Bravo into Mexico and started waylaying folks here and there, stealing what I needed, just trying to make a dollar or two..."

Brice rose, not interested in hearing more. He picked up the Winchester carbine Cato had given him to replace his own damaged weapon and wandered away some distance. Keeping his head low so as not to be potentially visible from below, Brice settled back against a rock that had been shaded through most of the day and thus felt deliciously cool through his sweat-soaked shirt. He looked over his grimy self, considering that he hadn't been this filthy and reeking since the war years. His bad leg ached, and he rubbed it.

"Mr. Brice?"

Orion had crept up on him unseen. It made him start—and also realize the natural stealth of the young man. Orion had the stance and grace of a natural outdoorsman; he seemed comfortable in these rugged barrens.

"Sit down, Orion. Keep your head down or Cato might shoot it off for fun."

"Yeah. He's a strange one. I still can't figure out why he didn't kill us."

"He might yet, or at least get us killed. I wonder how many will be in this cargo team we'll be jumping?"

"Hadn't thought about that."

Orion settled himself down with the effortlessness of a young cat. "Mr. Brice, is it stealing to take something a man has dropped?"

"I don't know. What are you talking about?"

"This." Orion reached into a pocket and pulled out Deguere's notebook. "Old Redbeard, he dropped this out of his riding jacket after the rocks and scrap fell on him down there. I kind of picked it up. I ain't the best for reading, but it looks to me like he's been lying to us. The name on it sure ain't Hugh Talbot."

Brice looked over the notebook. "Deguere. M. Deguere. Where have I heard that name?"

Brice read further. "Look at this, Orion. Records about my brother. The old wolf is after Simon. And here, look—'Payment received. W. Montrose, six hundred dollars.'" Brice slapped dust from his knee. "He's played me for a fool. Using you and me and what's happened to Keelan to get at Simon."

He flipped pages. "Look at this: 'June second—Detouring away from Wichita, hear from Washington office that bank robbery in St. Louis is thought to be Alianza crime. Murder of county judge in southern Illinois in newspapers. Also Alianza, government believes.'"

Brice skipped farther down.

"'August fifth—Little doubt now that Caine is going to visit brother. Also may visit old companion Strahan. Suspect Caine also to see Seahorn.

"'Seahorn working for Alianza, involved in several robberies. Bank robbery in Dallas possibly led by Seahorn underlings.'"

Brice stopped and closed the notebook. "I'm a fool, Orion. To think I accepted him as a government agent just because he said he was. What are we going to do about him?"

"Do? Go face-to-face with him, that's what!" Orion said. "Shoot him, if you need to. I'll do it! I'm already in trouble with the law as it is."

Brice firmly shook his head. "I won't murder a man nor see you do it. But once we get the dynamite, we break him off clean."

"I still say kill him."

At that moment one of Cato's gunmen gave a low whistle. Cato, who had seemed totally drunk before, now appeared to be stone sober. Deguere lifted his derby from his brow and slid over to the natural breastworks overlooking the enclosed pass. The atmosphere became tense.

"Look yonder," Orion whispered.

Coming in from the east was a line of packhorses, led by a line of riders. Eight men, it appeared.

They checked their rifles and waited. Suddenly the air seemed very still and hot.

Chapter 13

Ramon Fernandez wiped his mouth on his cuff and stood. He staggered, for he was drunk. Plunking money onto the table, he weaved out of the cantina.

Drunkenness was not characteristic of him, especially this early in the day. He drank mostly when having trouble with women, and at the moment the face of Rosalita Contero was all he could think about.

He hadn't really wanted to return her to the carcel, particularly to the same cell as Simon Caine. It had been rage that made him do it. Rage was the one force in his life that Ramon could not keep in check—it had been like that since the time when as a young man he had assaulted a village priest who criticized him for his habits. From that time on, it had been evident to Ramon that he was destined for something other than a life of following somebody else's rules.

He kept to the shade of the buildings as he walked. Some of the people who passed him spoke or nodded, but he ignored them. He fought the urge to free Rosalita once again from Seahorn's carcel. No. He wouldn't do it. She had scorned him, so let Seahorn have her. If he wanted, he could toss her to his two-legged animals for whatever fate they could dream up for her. Ramon didn't care. Wouldn't care.

He turned into an alley and sat down. He lit a small *cigarro* and let the smoke sooth him. He thought again of Neal Seahorn's safe full of money. When he had finished the *cigarro*, he stood, feeling a little more stable. Looking around the plaza, he realized how sick he was of this place. The

sun-blasted compound with its crumbling, century-old buildings and human-maggot inhabitants offended Ramon, who
had always thought himself more refined than the average
man. He decided on the spot that it was time to complete his
work and go.

Ramon thought it over. He had heard that soon, maybe
tonight, a shipment of weapons and whiskey was expected at
Serveto. Then there was the ransom for the kidnapped
boy—that should also be here soon. Ramon suspected that
when the ransom did arrive, Serveto would see the last of
Neal Seahorn and the contents of his safe. Unless, of course,
somebody else moved more quickly.

"Tonight," Ramon whispered up at Seahorn's window.
"Tonight we settle our debts."

He weaved off across the compound toward his own
quarters, ready to sleep.

For a small group, the Alianza weapons couriers put up a
valiant battle. But their efforts were futile against Cato's
brutal attack. Brice fired off three ineffective shots, then
stopped, feeling that somehow this ambush was wrong, even
if its victims were nothing but gunrunners and whiskey
traders in commerce with scum like Neal Seahorn. Orion
seemingly had no similar qualms, for Brice saw his tense
enthusiasm as he fought with the revolving Colt rifle—though
his shots seemed uncharacteristically inaccurate. Deguere
also joined Cato's attack eagerly, blasting at anything that
moved below him, and it was clear he was trying to connect.

As the battle progressed—much longer than Brice
expected—the narrow pass filled again with orange dust
mingled with gunsmoke. Several packhorses and burros,
laden with boxes and bundles covered with waterproof canvas, thrashed about and bucked in the confusion. They sent
up a ruckus of brays and trumpetings. The men who had
driven them sent up their own horrible wails, one by one, as
Cato's men picked them off.

We shouldn't have agreed to this, Brice thought. *That's a
massacre happening down there.*

Cato was perched about fifteen feet from Orion and

Brice on the rim of the pass wall. He stood now, carefully took aim, and fired a shot that brought a short, final-sounding shriek from below. Cato whooped like an Indian, enjoying his work.

Brice took a quick look below. Two men remained alive out of the original eight. One threw down his rifle and raised his hands. His companion shouted at him and kept on firing. Cato's band released another volley, and both of the men below fell. One lay still immediately, the other writhed for a moment until Cato pumped one more slug into him.

The pass suddenly grew quiet. Luminescent smoke and dust rose and dispersed. The burros, packhorses, and riderless mounts milled about, bumping each other, some of them escaping the pass, and then they, too, grew still.

Cato stood and let out another whoop. He raised his rifle above his head and shook it. At that moment he was the most clear image of pure savagery Brice had ever seen.

Already Cato's men were descending into the pass as quickly as they could. One leaped right over the drop and landed squarely in an empty saddle. The startled gelding beneath it trumpeted and bucked, throwing him off and drawing much laughter from his companions. The man rose, laughing, too, then did something that chilled Brice: He shot the gelding dead.

Lord above, get us out of here alive, Brice prayed. These are men who would help you one moment then blast out your brains the next.

Deguere was standing, smiling at Brice and Orion. "Quite a battle, eh?" he exulted.

"More like murder," Brice returned.

"Come now, my friend! Exterminating desert vermin is a high calling. This is war! Aren't we fighting to get back your son?"

"I am. You're not," Brice said.

Deguere looked puzzled, maybe even a little concerned by that remark, but he had no time to inquire. Cato shouted at them from below, waving whiskey bottles in each hand.

"Good whiskey, *amigos*! Join the celebration!"

"I don't want whiskey," Brice said. "Just dynamite."

He, Orion, and Deguere descended a southward slope that led them gradually back into the pass. The bloody bodies, lying with eyes and mouths open, were terrible to see. A scorpion skittered across the shattered forehead of one of the dead men. Already turkey vultures circled above.

Cato was still trying to push whiskey on his new friends, and Brice finally accepted a bottle to humor him. He took one small swallow, but he was in no mood to drink.

"Where's the dynamite?" Deguere asked Cato.

One of Cato's Mexicans ran up to him, dangerous-looking blasting sticks in hand. He dropped one; Brice thought he would not get his breath back again for at least ten seconds.

"*Dinamita!*" shouted the exuberant Mexican. "Blow Serveto into hell!"

"Not to mention us, unless you exercise a bit more care, my friend," Deguere said as he gingerly took the dynamite. "Much more?"

"*Muy dinamita.* Three men make an army with *dinamita.*"

"Indeed."

"Come aside. I want to talk to you," Brice said to Deguere.

"Certainly." Deguere was carefully placing the blasting sticks into his pockets and spoke inattentively.

"I think maybe you lost this—Mr. Deguere." Brice held up the notebook.

Deguere's expression became stern. "Where did you—"

"I ought to kill you, Mr. Deguere. Kill you and leave you for the buzzards. I've heard your name before. Just who are you?"

Deguere looked sincerely stunned. He seemed to be faltering about for a lie, then he stopped. His words came with the flat sound of truth.

"So you've caught me. I'm a detective, and I work for William Montrose."

"You're after Simon."

"I'm after money. Whether it comes from Montrose in reward for your brother's death or if it comes from elsewhere makes no difference to me."

"Elsewhere?"

"Serveto. There must be great wealth there. I figured that by accompanying you I could possibly get my hands on it. If not, at least I might complete my job for Montrose. It was worth a try."

Brice drew back his fist and pounded it into Deguere's mouth. The lip split and blood poured into Deguere's auburn beard. Deguere shook his head as if to clear it, touched his lip, but otherwise seemed unaffected, even unangered.

"I suppose I deserve that, from your viewpoint."

"You deserve castration," Brice said. "What would you have done once we got into Serveto? Turned us over to Neal Seahorn to get his favor and maybe his money?"

Deguere lifted a finger. "Now, that's an idea I hadn't thought of. You've a devious brain, my friend. Actually, I was really ready to help you if I could, as long as I could pursue my own quest in Serveto as well. I'm not heartless, you know—the idea of a kidnapped boy is most unpleasant."

Brice was so angry speaking was difficult. "You're a lucky man, Deguere. If I were my brother, I'd be taking your scalp right here. But I'm more merciful—I'll let you ride out, and as long as I never see you again, you'll be safe from me. If I do see you, you die. Whenever, wherever."

Deguere had produced a handkerchief and was using it to staunch the blood flow from his lip. It slightly muffled his voice. "Come now—don't you see I can still be of use to you? I'm still as capable as I ever was. And what do you care what happens to Simon Caine?"

"Keep talking and I'll gut you."

"All right. I'll give you my word: I'll not harm Simon Caine—if he's alive, which I doubt—and I'll do all I can to help you free your son. All I want is a fair crack at Seahorn's money. It's a long shot, certainly, but worth the trying. You've got my word."

"Your word is so much spit. Get out of my sight. And leave that dynamite here. We need it all."

Deguere shook his head. "Well, it was a good effort." He straightened his derby. "Gentlemen, it's been too brief a pleasure, and I'm sorry it has come to this. You need not worry about seeing me again, Mr. James. You will not survive your mission, I fully believe. With my help perhaps you could have." He smiled coldly. "Perhaps I can go to work for Seahorn later. I think he might need a good gravedigger. One who can dig holes sufficient for grown fools—and perhaps one just the size for the corpse of a boy."

Brice was on Deguere then, his fury coursing into his arms like blood through his veins. He hit Deguere again, again, but the bearded man expertly swept him off. He deftly kicked two times, knocking Brice to the dirt. Orion lifted his rifle, but before it was leveled, Deguere was pointing a derringer into the handsome black face.

"Don't be just another dead nigger," he said. He laughed in contempt, lowered the derringer, and walked away, and Orion, somehow, could not summon the nerve to shoot him.

Chapter 14

Under the cover of falling darkness, Brice and Orion slipped unseen through the rocky notch of Puerta de Serveto. Above them the western sky clung to the last fading traces of a rich crimson sunset, as if reluctant to give in to the darkness. And the darkness would be deep tonight, for the clouds were pouring over the horizon and piling themselves thick against the sky. Thunder sounded, the wind kicked up, and the two travelers knew they were about to be struck by the fury of a rare desert storm.

As they led their mounts through the pass on hooves muffled with cloth wrappings, Brice felt his heart pound in his chest and his blood surge in his temples. Serveto lay just ahead, and in there, somewhere, was Keelan.

Being this close to his son did strange things to his emotions. He experienced both an intense longing for his son and a deep grief for him. He also missed Agatha terribly and wished he could touch her for a moment to gather strength for the coming ordeal.

They had abandoned the packhorses a mile back, but on Brice's horse was strapped a box with several sticks of dynamite. More than enough, Brice figured, to blow much of Serveto off its century-old foundations. And God help him, he would love to do just that if he could—after Keelan was safe.

"Mr. Brice?"

"What?"

"You got any idea how to get into that place?"

"Cato said there is some sort of stream running through a grate at the northern wall, up against the hills. Maybe we can get through there some way."

Lightning arched across the sky, followed by a jolting round of thunder. Brice's horse whinnied and almost spooked.

"Whoa, boy. Calm down." Brice stopped. Deep sadness came over him. He turned to Orion.

"I can't have you go through with this," he said. "I have no real plan, no good chance of succeeding. I'm doing this because it's my boy in there, and I've got to. You should turn back while you can."

"Like I told you before, Mr. Brice. That was my pa they kilt."

Brice nodded. "All right. But you know that—"

"That we probably won't come back? Yeah, I know it. What does it matter for me? I've kilt now, and there's nothing but a rockpile or a noose for me—or just the trail and looking over my shoulder the rest of my days."

Brice said, "You're a friend, Orion. Best kind a man could have."

Orion seemed uncomfortable with the praise. "We'd best keep going," he said.

They went on farther, winding along the trail. The wind rose and fell. They topped a rise just as a big flash of lightning cracked the sky from end to end. By its light they saw it: the town of Serveto, the big walled former misson and presidio looming in its center. To Brice it looked like a vast prison, gray and oppressive.

"God help us," he said, for the sight made him and Orion and their few handfuls of dynamite seem insignificant and helpless, like ants assaulting a bank safe.

Orion seemed to be having similar thoughts. He stood quietly, staring across at the seeming fortress.

"We're never even going to get in, Mr. Brice," he said hopelessly.

"I'll get in," Brice said. "I'll get in even if I have to scratch down the wall with my fingernails."

Lightning flashed again and it started to rain.

* * *

Neal Seahorn watched the rising storm from his window and tossed down another glass of tequila. *Edgy tonight. Nervous about something—don't know what . . .*

Yet he did know. And he wished heartily that he had fled earlier in the day, simply run out rather than sit here and wait for the inevitable coming of Ramon.

He looked at his empty glass. His hand shook, blast it, shook like that of a doting old man! He slammed down the glass, angry at himself.

Why was he so afraid of Ramon? Was Neal Seahorn not the equal of any man in a fight?

At one time, maybe. Now, maybe not. He was growing older, though he disliked admitting it. How long had it been since he squarely faced a man in a gunfight? Or even in a fist-and-knuckle brawl? What Neal Seahorn was afraid of tonight was the unknown, and in this case, the unknown was himself.

The rain began, a sweeping storm that would pound the plaza into mud and wash red silt from the hills down through the gullies and gulches. A storm to drive everyone in Serveto inside their quarters . . .

Suddenly he realized it: he hadn't missed his best opportunity to leave Serveto after all. Nature was giving it to him right now. But he must move quickly. He went to a wardrobe and brought out saddlebags, which he stuffed with clothing, what food he had about, ammunition, and other goods. Then he opened the door into the hallway that led to the room where his safe stood.

When he knelt and began working the lock, he had a moment of doubt. If he double-crossed the Alianza, he would not be forgiven nor forgotten. They would look for him, they would find him, and he would die. The Alianza was a rattler with no rattles, and it could strike him when he was not expecting it.

He refused to think about it. Since when did Neal Seahorn run from any man or organization? And who could find Seahorn when he did not wish to be found?

But they found Simon Caine, he remembered. Found him when the federal government could not.

The heavy safe door creaked open and Seahorn saw the stacks of bills in the safe. He forgot his fears then and knew he was doing the right thing. Outside the storm grew louder; he could hear the rain driving against the thick-tiled roof. That was good—he would leave no tracks in such a storm.

A shadow, a subtle sound. Seahorn felt something like ice against his spine. Slowly he turned.

Ramon was very drunk. That Seahorn could see at once. The handsome Mexican stood, drenched from the storm, and toyed with his pistol, repeatedly turning the cylinder.

"*Salud,* Neal. I have come to kill you."

Seahorn stood. He gulped, and it was like swallowing sand. "You're drunk, Ramon. You don't want to do this. Go home."

"No. No."

"Where is Rosalita?"

"Don't speak of her. You have made a blunder, Neal. You sent a fool like Fadden to do a job too big for him—and that is too bad for you, for now it is you who must die."

Ramon's bloodshot eyes drifted for a second to the open safe. "You were leaving, maybe? Taking the money with you?"

Seahorn's mind desperately searched for some scheme. "You always did see right through me, Ramon. Perhaps I was wrong about you. I'm glad Fadden didn't succeed. Listen—we can be partners, closer than ever before. You take half the money, I take half—"

"No. First you die, then I take it all."

Seahorn stared coldly at him. "You want the money, then take it. Here—I'll even get it out for you."

He knelt at the safe, turning his back on Ramon. He was risking a backshot, but he had a good reason: a loaded Remington pistol he had hidden beneath the stack of cash as a precaution.

"There is enough here for both of us, Ramon," Seahorn said. "I hope you'll reconsider—"

Still crouched, he spun. The Remington blasted, deafeningly loud. Ramon pitched back against the wall, stood there for a moment, and then his pistol dropped to the floor and he slowly slid down, leaving a red trail all the way down. The bullet had passed completely through him.

The wall at which Brice and Orion stood was thick and tall, impossible to scale, but near one corner there was a narrow channel through which a small wet-weather stream ran. The builders of the Serveto presidio had not diverted it because it provided easy water for livestock, and so it remained. The channel was, in effect, a tunnel through the wall, but in its midst was a barrier of crossed iron bars.

Despite the rain, the water in the stream was no more than ten inches deep at the moment, a muddy swirl that drenched Orion as he knelt in the passage and sought to work loose enough of the rusty bars to let himself through.

Brice hugged the wall outside, looking about for sentries. Every flash of lightning made him feel exposed. But he was grateful for the storm, too; it had apparently driven the guards from the walls and now covered the noise Orion made at his work.

Brice noticed the stream beginning to rise. He knelt and whisper-called in to his partner, "Any luck yet?"

As if in answer, Orion heaved back. A metallic wrenching noise heralded the removal of the first iron bar. The young man turned, grinning, and showed it to Brice.

"Good," Brice said. "How much more?"

"Couple more bars and we can squeeze under the bottom."

He went back to his task, tugging at the ancient metal. The second bar came off easier than the first. He started pulling on a third.

"Water's rising," Brice whispered in.

Orion had been too busy to notice, but now he saw Brice was right. The water reached almost to his waist as he knelt.

He worked with greater vigor. At last the iron bar gave a moaning creak of surrender and pulled away in his hand. One end, though, remained attached. No time to break it loose; Orion put his weight against it and bent it back as far as possible.

He looked over his shoulder to where Brice peered at him at the end of the channel.

"I'm going under—you shift in the dynamite," he said. He took a lungful of air and disappeared under the water.

In a moment he appeared on the other side, soaked but smiling. Brice smiled, too. Success so far—they had found a workable entrance into Serveto.

Brice picked up the box of dynamite, covered in canvas, and waded in a stoop back into the tunnel. At the grate barrier he said, "Pull it up as fast as you can, and try to get the water out. This may ruin some of it."

He submerged the box and pushed it through the opening Orion had made. It was a tight fit, but sufficient. Orion brought up the box on the other side, quickly removed it from the protective canvas cover, and drained the little bit of water that had leaked in.

"Appears to be all right," he said.

Brice went back out and picked up their rifles and sidearms. These he passed to Orion through the grate.

Brice said, "Slip on out into the compound, find a place to hide. I'm coming through."

Balancing the box of dynamite and the weapons with difficulty, Orion crouch-walked to the inside mouth of the water channel. Brice saw him outlined there against the backdrop of the rain-battered grounds of Serveto, then he moved out and to the right.

Brice was on his knees in the stream and the water was up past his waist. He filled his lungs with air and descended. Beneath the dark, swirling water he could see nothing. He groped for the grate, found it, and began pulling himself through.

The storm seemed to give a massive shudder and cast off sweeping sheets of water. The hills outside Serveto belched out gushes of brown liquid. The passageway all but filled even as Brice struggled through the opening.

He was broader in the chest and stomach than Orion, and he barely fit the hole. Holding his breath, he fought to pull through, but it took a long time. His brain began to spin, stars to burst beneath his eyelids. *No, not like this. Don't let me drown this close to finding Keelan. Don't end it like this—*

Orion was becoming concerned. He had emerged into

what appeared to be a large, empty livestock pen. He was hiding behind a small stable about five yards from the mouth of the water passage. The stream ran through the pen, filled nearly to the top.

And Brice still had not emerged.

He heard a shot—muffled, and coming from the other side of the compound. He heard a voice calling, then another. The shot had apparently drawn attention. It might generate investigation, men in the compound, sentries back on the walls.

Still no Brice. Orion swore and put down his weapons. He ran back to the channel mouth and looked in.

He saw nothing but blackness vomiting out water. He could not see Brice at all.

"Mr. Brice?"

Suddenly there was movement nearby. He spun. A man was moving across the compound on the other side of the stone wall that formed one portion of this stock enclosure. Orion saw the up-and-down movement of his hat above the edge of that wall.

Though frustrated and fearful for Brice's life, he had no choice but to scurry back behind the stable. Voices. Two men there now, and coming this way.

Orion picked up the weapons and the dynamite and moved along the back of the stable to its far side. There the pen wall was broken and low. He crossed it, entering a little grove of trees. He vanished into the shadows.

Chapter 15

Caine held up the sharpened piece of metal and examined it critically. Then he nodded in satisfaction. He had found the scrap beneath the straw on the floor, and he had patiently worked it to a point against the stone. Rosalita had altered between watching him work and watching the storm outside the barred window.

"You will kill the guard with that?" she asked.

"Nope," Caine said. "I doubt I'd get close enough to him. The point is for you to kill yourself."

"What?" Her expression almost made Caine laugh.

"Look, if we're to share the same cell, you might as well call me Simon—not that I intend either of us to be in this cell much longer. Don't worry, you won't really kill yourself. You'll just threaten to, very loud and very sincere."

Rosalita tried to surmise his plan. "But why would the guards try to stop me? Why would they care?"

"They may not. But I'm going to try to make them."

"And then?"

"Let's skin this bear before we tackle the next one. You get back into that corner, where they'll have to come all the way in to get you. Put the sharp part to your neck...wait a minute." Caine probed his arm with the point and drew blood. He let a little of it pool on his arm.

"Smear some of that on your neck and touch the point there," he said. "Makes it more convincing. And you've got to sound completely plumb stark loco, else they won't buy it. Understand?"

She nodded as she dabbed some of Caine's blood at her throat. She crossed herself, took the sharp bar, and went to the corner. There she looked back at Caine.

"Go to it," he said.

Her first scream was enough to convince even Caine she was in utter despair. She gave another, and another, and began babbling Spanish words Caine could not understand.

The guards appeared at the door, looking through the little window. One of them shouted at Rosalita, but she continued crying out, probing the sharp point into her throat.

Caine waved at her. "Aren't you going to stop her? She's ready to carve out her own throat!"

The guards looked disturbed and uncertain. One ordered Rosalita to stop, but Caine laughed.

"She's given up—figures she's going to die a worse death if she doesn't do it herself."

One of the guards said, "Well, what does it matter? No one will care if she lives."

Caine laughed. "You're a fool, then. Neal Seahorn and Ramon Fernandez both love that woman—the only reason she's in here now is that they're too busy fighting over her to know what to do with her. She dies, you'll die."

Rosalita gave a particularly startling scream. Caine was amazed to see her actually cut the skin of her throat a little. Fresh blood flowed down her neck.

The guards mumbled between themselves, then opened the door. One of them went to Rosalita; the other lifted his rifle and covered Caine.

Rosalita then did something Caine had not anticipated— she jabbed the blade deep into the arm of the guard closest to her. He screeched and leaped back. He examined the bleeding wound, cursed Rosalita, and raised his rifle.

The stabbing had distracted the guard covering Caine just enough to allow Caine to reach him a second before he would have shot Rosalita. Caine pulled the rifle away. The other guard saw it and spun away from Rosalita toward Caine. Rosalita lunged forward again, this time driving the sharp metal bit deep into the guard's side. He collapsed, then a moment later died.

The other guard, now weaponless, fell on his knees and begged Caine for mercy. Caine pounded the butt of the rifle into the man's forehead, and he fell unconscious. Caine stripped the shirts from the guards and with them tied up the survivor.

"Come on!" Caine urged.

He gave Rosalita the first guard's rifle. He dug in their pockets for spare ammunition and found only a little, but he also discovered a loaded double-barreled derringer, which he gave to Rosalita. She dropped it into the pocket of her dress.

Caine and Rosalita entered the hallway of the makeshift carcel. A ring of keys hung at the far end, and Caine got it. He went to Keelan's cell, fumbled the lock open, pushed the door open.

"Come on, son, it's time—"

He stared in surprise into an empty cell. Keelan was gone.

Caine spun on his heel and went back to the tied-up guard. He picked him up by the collar and slapped at his face until he came to.

"Where is the boy?" he demanded.

The Mexican talked as if his tongue were too thick for his mouth. "Seahorn . . . came . . . took him."

Caine let go of the man's collar, and the back of his head thumped against the stone floor, knocking him unconscious once more.

"But why would Seahorn take him?" Rosalita asked.

"I should have known he would do something like that. He'll probably try to ransom the boy off himself and take the money for his own."

"So he betrays the Alianza?"

"Betrayal," Caine said, "is in Neal Seahorn's blood."

There were two of them, and they found Brice floating facedown in the muddy, foaming water that gushed in through the wall channel. One of them, a tall Anglo, pulled him out and rolled him over. He leaned his ear to his chest.

"Alive," he told the bandoliered Mexican with him. "Seahorn will want to know of this."

"Yep." The Anglo disarmed Brice, stood, and hefted him onto his shoulder like a sack of oats. The pair, like several others, had come out into the rain to investigate what had sounded like a muffled gunshot somewhere in the enclosure. They had not found its origin, but what they had found here was much more interesting. And perhaps a source of reward from Seahorn.

The Anglo and the Mexican reached Seahorn's quarters and climbed the stairs; the Mexican reached the door first and knocked on it.

No one answered, so he knocked again. A moment later the door creaked slowly open, and both the Anglo and the Mexican stepped back in surprise.

Ramon Fernandez stood before them, his usually swarthy face almost drained of color. Blood, a lot of it, soaked his clothing. He wobbled on his feet, clinging to the door.

"Seahorn has killed me," he said, just before he collapsed.

The Mexican knelt beside him, felt him. He looked up at his partner, his brown eyes wide. "He is dead," he said.

The Anglo looked wildly around. Suddenly he dumped Brice's unconscious form on the floor beside Ramon's corpse. "Let's get out of here," he said.

Brice lay still for several more minutes. Water slowly drained from his lungs and spilled out of his mouth, and his shuddering, weak breathing steadily became stronger. Color began returning, and at last he opened his eyes.

Slowly he pushed himself up, until he saw the dead man beside him. He looked around, utterly confused. How had he come here, wherever here was? The last thing he could recall was struggling beneath the water, trying to squeeze through the opening at the bottom of the iron grate.

He stood, holding the wall, until his strength returned. He assessed his situation. He guessed he was somewhere inside Serveto. Had he wandered here in a daze? Or had he been carried here—by whom? And where was Orion?

He examined the body on the floor. A finely dressed Mexican, shot through the chest. Apparently the man had bled to death.

Brice looked around the hallway, dimly lit by a lamp on

the wall. A door stood open behind the dead Mexican. Brice carefully peered inside. A living quarters, it appeared. Nicely furnished, too, with overstuffed chairs, a big table, a large sideboard, paintings on the wall. He listened and heard no movement inside. He stepped across the Mexican's body and entered.

A trail of blood showed where the bleeding man had moved across the room to the door. He followed the trail back to another doorway leading into another hallway. Brice walked into it, wondering if maybe Keelan was somewhere in this building. His foot struck something on the floor. A pistol. He picked it up. The grip was slick with blood. The Mexican must have dropped the pistol from his weakening fingers as he came down this hallway.

Brice passed down the hall and entered the room at its end. A safe stood there, open and empty.

There was nothing else in the room, so Brice turned and went back into the main chamber. There were two more doors. One led into another long passage; the smell of food drifted up it to him. A kitchen beyond, probably. The other door, though, led into a bedroom.

This, too, was empty. The bed was rumpled and un-made. Clothing hung in an open wardrobe against the far wall. Brice went to it, examining what it held. He noticed a gunbelt hanging from a peg inside. No pistol, just an empty holster. But then he saw the name neatly etched into the leather: N. Seahorn.

This was Seahorn's room. The room of the very man who held Keelan captive.

Brice took one of Seahorn's shirts and wiped the blood from the pistol and his hands. He spat contemptuously into the wardrobe, then at the bed where Seahorn had slept.

Tucking the pistol under his own belt, he went back into the main room. There he blew out the lamps that burned here and there, and in the darkness he went to the tall window that opened onto a balcony.

He was in Serveto, all right. Below him spread the plaza, still being pounded with rain. Lightning showed him various buildings here and there, their shapes rectangular and stark as they were limned for a second against the backlighting sky.

He studied each building, hoping for some clue to indicate where his son might be held. But he found no sign. He saw two men move across the plaza and ducked farther inside Seahorn's room.

It struck him that he should quickly get out of here. Seahorn might return at any moment.

Brice headed back to the hall, but he heard voices. After looking frantically about, he darted into Seahorn's room again and slipped into the big wardrobe. Pulling the clothing around him, he eased the door almost shut. Through the open space he could see just a bit into the main room.

"He's dead, all right," a man said. "You didn't see who did it?"

"No. But Seahorn is gone. He was seen running across the plaza toward the carcel, and since then he has vanished. I have heard that somewhere here he has a safe full of money. I'll bet it's empty now."

"But why would Seahorn shoot Ramon?"

"Haven't you heard what's gone on?" a voice with a Mexican accent said. "They say Ramon and Seahorn fought over Rosalita Contero, and then Seahorn sent J. W. Fadden to kill Ramon. Ramon killed Fadden instead—and now it seems Seahorn has done the same to Ramon."

A pause, then one said, "If Seahorn has run off, he's probably taken everything for himself. Our wages, too, I'll bet."

"Well, then there is nothing holding us anymore—and no reason for us not to take what we can find."

Brice watched through the opening; he saw forms moving about as the men talked.

"And what of the kidnapped boy? Who will collect his ransom?"

Brice closed his eyes and breathed a prayer of gratitude for the indication Keelan was still alive.

"Maybe we will," one of the men said. "The ransom is due at any time."

"Well, I don't plan to hang around waiting for no ransom

or anything else. Think about it—maybe Seahorn took off because he knew something bad was about to happen. There may be a passel of rangers crossing the border. Or the whole damn Mex army."

"That's right," one of the others said. "Let's take what we can find and leave. Let's look for that safe of Seahorn's. Might be something left in it."

Brice tried not to breathe as the men began searching the rooms. One of the men did come into the bedroom and begin looking about, moving pictures, shoving aside the bed. Then he walked toward the wardrobe. Brice saw his face clearly through the opening, and his hand extending—

"We found it!" one of the others called.

The man turned and quickly left the bedroom. Brice exhaled a long, relieved sigh.

Chapter 16

Caine could almost smell a difference in the atmosphere of Serveto. The place simply felt different. Neal Seahorn's absence was as tangible here as the moisture that hung in the air as the storm finally gave out.

Caine and Rosalita moved along the base of the wall, hugging it close, letting the shadows swallow them. From the carcel they ran toward a row of empty adobe houses, around the back of the old mission chapel. From there they cut toward Rosalita's adobe house, dangerously exposed to view.

Someone shouted nearby, and a shot was fired. Caine at first thought they had been seen, but an exultant whoop followed, then three more shots in succession. He saw the gunman—someone firing at the sky.

"What is happening?" Rosalita asked.

"Word is probably spreading that Seahorn has gone," Caine said. "Serveto is about to come apart. If we're found here, they might buy us a drink, or they might kill us. I'd bet on the latter: a lot of men would like to say they brought me down. Then there's the price tag on my head."

They reached Rosalita's house. Rosalita went to the door and started to open it, but Caine motioned for her to stop. The she heard it, too: someone inside. Moving, knocking things about.

"Looting," Caine whispered. "The door through the outside wall—is it still open?"

"I don't know."

"Come on. We'll try it."

They ran across the plaza. While they were in the open, men emerged from various buildings. Caine heard angry shouts; someone cursed Seahorn's name.

If Caine and Rosalita were seen, they were not noticed, for no one reacted to them. They darted into the tree-shaded alley and through to the little door through the wall—and found it sealed shut.

"I figured they would have done that," Caine said. "Any way out besides the front gate?"

"Nothing but over the wall."

Caine looked up. The wall was twelve feet high, and its smooth stone surface offered no handholds.

"I'll find something to climb on," he said.

An empty barrel stood against the wall farther down, and Caine went to it. As he touched it, a shot blasted somewhere nearby and a slug knocked chips out of the wall inches from him.

Caine wheeled, pumped two shots from his rifle in the general direction from which the slug had come, then shouted for Rosalita to run. She did.

"It's Caine!" someone yelled. "He's loose!"

More shots, more slugs chipping the wall, digging the dirt at Caine's heels. He ran to his right, then cut between the rows of adobes again. A shading overhang, or *portal*, was built onto one of the adobes, and beneath it was a plank porch built about eighteen inches above the ground. Caine dropped to his belly and slid under the porch. Moments later he watched three pairs of boots stomp by as his pursuers went after him.

Something touched his hand, and he started. It was Rosalita. He exhaled in relief.

"Lucky I didn't put my fist through your face," he said. "I didn't know you were under here."

"There was nowhere else."

"I got to get you out of here."

"How?"

"Hush!"

Some had stepped onto the porch. The clunk of the boots was loud. Caine and Rosalita hardly breathed. Two men above.

"Got away," one said. "But he couldn't have got over the wall."

"Then let's keep looking."

"Forget Caine," the first responded. "Go after Seahorn. Get back the money he took, and the boy, Garth Kensington would pay a lot to get the boy back. That's why Seahorn took him. I figure the kid to be worth more than Caine."

"Maybe so. But the storm will have washed over Seahorn's trail," the other said. "By morning he'll have such a jump we'd have a hard time catching up to him. But Caine's inside these walls, and we ought to be able to spook him out. Let's give it a try."

The other grunted apparent assent and the men moved away. Caine shook his head. Always it was the same—having either to hide for his own protection, and if not hide, to kill.

"There's got to be some other way out of here," he said to Rosalita. "Think hard."

Rosalita concentrated. "There is a passage for the stream. It is dry except when it rains—I think it is blocked."

"It's worth trying," Caine said.

Carefully they crawled out from under the porch. Men still moved about the plaza, and it was impossible for the pair to remain fully hidden. Fortunately, Caine realized, either not everyone here was aware of who he was, or if they were, did not care, so he and Rosalita moved along without being molested.

Near the stone armory Caine saw two men moving together, and something about them made him suspect they were the two who had been on the porch moments before. Though they apparently did not see him now, Caine and Rosalita were dangerously in the open.

On impulse, Caine tried the armory door. He was surprised to find it unlocked. He went inside and pulled Rosalita after him, then closed the door almost completely.

The two men walked nearby; one looked directly at the armory. But they did not stop.

When they were gone, Caine turned. He was going to tell Rosalita they could go on now, but he found himself staring into the black muzzle of a long revolving Colt rifle held by a very intense-eyed young black man.

"You twitch and you die," the man said.

"I won't twitch," Caine said.

The man lowered the Colt rifle a bit. "You look like somebody I know," he said. "Who are you?"

"What does that matter?"

The rifle came up again.

"My name is Robert Cole."

"Why you come in here?"

"To save my hide. There's some men after me."

The black man suddenly looked at Caine very intently, cocking his head slightly to the side. "You're Simon Caine," he said. "I know because you look like Mr. Brice."

Caine couldn't mask his surprise. "You know my brother?"

"Yeah. I come here with him to get his boy. My name's Orion Jones."

"Where is he?"

Worry skirted across Orion's face. "I think he's dead."

Caine felt as if he were sinking into deep water. "How?"

"We come in the place where the water flows in through the wall. There's metal bars there—I think he got hung up under the water. Men come along run me off before I could help him loose."

Through Caine's mind flashed memories of his brother as a child, as a young man, and as he had seen him last, atop the stone tower near the Kensington ranch. Emotion threatened to overcome him, but he dammed it up and swallowed it down. "Who are you, Orion?"

"Me and my pa worked for Mr. Kensington and Mr. Brice. My pa, he got shot dead by them what kidnapped Mr. Brice's boy."

"Orion, this is Rosalita Contero. She and I were locked up by Neal Seahorn—Keelan was in the same place."

"Where is Keelan now?"

"Seahorn took him and left Serveto. That's why there's all the stir outside. Seahorn robbed the place blind, and hell's busted loose."

"I want to get Keelan back—for Mr. Brice," Orion said.

"We'll do it together."

Orion nodded.

"What do we do now, Simon?" Rosalita asked.

"Well, we at least got plenty of weaponry," he said, looking around.

"I got dynamite," Orion said.

"How'd you get—"

"It's a long story."

"Tell me later, then. Just bring the stuff out."

Brice watched the growing commotion in Serveto and didn't know what to make of it. Men moving about, doors and windows being smashed, goods being strewn across the plaza, looting going on everywhere. At first it dismayed him—how could he find Keelan in this turmoil?—but then he realized the hubbub might be an advantage, for in it he could probably move unnoticed.

But he wished he had some weapon besides the blood-stained pistol he had found on the dead Mexican. And he still wondered what had happened to Orion.

Brice stepped out into the plaza. He felt dangerously exposed, but the men who passed him, carrying items taken from one of the adobes, did not even glance at him. Nor did the horsemen a dozen yards away who were chasing down a hefty, screaming woman they had apparently driven from her home. Their intent Brice could guess.

He crossed the plaza, holding his pistol, not knowing where to go. It was almost funny, he thought. All his worry about entering Serveto, about remaining hidden and safe once here—and now he was walking openly through the heart of it.

A man stumbled by, several bottles of liquor under his arm. He apparently had already partaken of much of it, for he smiled cordially at Brice and extended a bottle. Brice ignored the offer but asked, "The prisoners . . . where does Seahorn keep the prisoners?"

The drunk slurred out, "Yonder. But they're all gone. Empty."

Brice felt an inward lurch of dismay. "The boy?"

"The kidnapped one? Everybody says Seahorn took him for hisself and run off."

"Run off . . ."

"Yep." The drunk turned and weaved away, turning up his bottle as he went. Brice stood there, hands hanging at his side, and felt as if he could not move. Suddenly he turned and trotted after the drunk. He grabbed the man's shoulder. One of the bottles beneath his arm fell and broke.

"Hey! What are you—"

"Simon Caine—is he alive?"

"Live as you or me. I ought to kill you—you broke my bottle." The man weaved off.

Suddenly the door of a nearby stone building swung open, pushed from inside. Brice spun, instinctively raising his rifle.

It was equally instinctive when Simon Caine fired at the figure before him. Through the blast of his rifle's fire and smoke he saw the man jerk and fall. An unexplainable feeling of sickness suddenly swept over Caine.

Orion cried out, "It's Mr. Brice! You shot him!" He ran to the still form on the ground and knelt by him.

Caine leaned against the door, his legs suddenly weak beneath him. After a moment he went to his brother.

"Brice? I didn't know it was you..."

Brice opened his eyes. "Keelan," he said. "Where is..." He fell unconscious.

Caine stood and breathed deeply. A man with a gun darted around a nearby corner; Caine caught a glint of gunmetal. Caine spun, lifted his rifle, and shot the man through the heart. He walked to the body and picked up a lighted cigar that had fallen from the man's lips. Caine dusted it off and put it in his own mouth.

"The dynamite, Orion," he said.

Orion knew, as he watched the destruction of Serveto, that never again would he see a fury like this. They had moved Brice to the relative safety of an alleyway, and then Caine had walked into the plaza, sticks of dynamite stuffed into each pocket and beneath his belt.

The first stick he cast into Seahorn's quarters, and it blasted out the full-length window and the wall around it. In the night the explosion was strangely beautiful, an eerie blossom of sparks bursting out in magnificent destruction.

Two men rose from behind a wagon, leveling rifles on Caine. Orion was about to shout a warning when Caine lit another fuse with his cigar, turned, and threw the stick directly under the wagon. Orion averted his eyes as the blast splintered the wagon and killed the men behind it.

On Caine continued, seemingly untouchable there in the plaza, throwing dynamite wherever he went, downing buildings, destroying stables and barns and walls. The few who dared try to stop him failed, fatally, and finally Serveto seemed to empty, so that Caine was left unchallenged. Orion and Rosalita watched him silently, a lone figure in the broad plaza that now was lighted with leaping flames.

"He is an amazing man, no?" Rosalita said.

"He is, ma'am. The most amazing I've ever seen."

And then it was done. Caine strode back to them, knelt again beside Brice. Brice's eyes moved, lids lifting for a moment, then falling again.

"I'll get the boy back for you, brother," Caine said. "Don't you die. I'll get him back."

An hour later they rode out of Serveto, Brice lying on a horse-drawn litter. Caine rode slightly ahead of Orion, who noted two remaining sticks of dynamite sticking out of Caine's pocket.

"What's those for?" he asked.

"Seahorn."

"How will we find him?"

"We?"

"Yeah. I'm going with you."

"We'll find him."

"But we don't know where he's heading."

Caine said, "I know. He's heading for the Big Bend country to find a Mexican called Old Pablo."

Chapter 17

Days and miles away from Serveto, Rosalita Contero stood in the doorway of a bedroom and watched Brice as he lay slightly propped up in bed, staring out the window. Before him lay a plate of food, barely touched.

"Do you need anything else?" Rosalita asked. Without looking at her, Brice shook his head.

Rosalita took the plate. She scraped the scraps out the door, where three scrawny dogs immediately devoured them. A plump Mexican woman, Rosalita's sister and the owner of this *casa*, stood at an oven outside, poking the fire as she prepared to bake bread. Rosalita took the plate back into the house and immersed it in a big crockery basin filled with water. She then went back out to her sister.

Rosalita and Brice had been here almost two weeks now. Her sister, the widowed, impoverished, and very plump Ria de Velasco, had freely opened her home to Rosalita and Brice despite having not seen her roving younger sister for the past seven years.

Ria had asked Rosalita what had become of her husband, Juan, of whom she had not approved, and when Rosalita told her simply that he had been killed, Ria nodded as if she had expected that answer. She had pointed a stubby finger at Brice and said in a too-loud whisper that this one, Rosalita, looks much better for you. We will take good care of him, no?

Yes, we will, Rosalita had said, and she had realized the idea was appealing. Brice was a fine-looking man, like his brother, and seemingly a good one. Ready to die in the effort to retrieve his son—that impressed Rosalita, for she had seen too little of love and loyalty in the circles in which she had run these past years.

Rosalita approached her sister, wiping her arm across her forehead as she bent over the round-topped oven. The house was surrounded by a handful of outbuildings, including one small building that Ria called her *granero*, or barn, though it hardly was big enough to merit the designation. Around the little enclave rose rocky Texas hills. Miles northward stretched the Sierra Diablo, and to the northeast, the Delaware Mountains.

"So again he did not eat?" Ria asked.

"No."

"Ah, that's bad. Bad. Why does he waste himself away so?"

"Because his son is still captive and he can only lie in bed while others go after him," Rosalita said. "It is hard for him to do that, and hard for him to be unable to walk."

"It will go bad for the boy," Ria said, shaking her head. "They say Neal Seahorn is a man without mercy. If the boy angers him—"

"Don't talk so, Ria. I don't want to hear it."

Ria smiled in a self-depreciating way. "Talk, talk, that is all I do. Pay no attention to me, *hermana*."

Rosalita walked away, glum and a little angry. Angry not at Ria's words, but at the fact she probably was right.

She had not, at the beginning, understood why Seahorn had taken Brice's son with him when he fled Serveto, but Simon Caine had surmised it was because the boy might be a useful hostage if Seahorn were cornered by the law. Furthermore, he said, Seahorn could now hold Keelan James as his own prisoner, demanding a new ransom.

Caine and Orion had ridden off in search of Seahorn and Keelan just as quickly as Brice and Rosalita were settled in at the widowed Ria's home. Rosalita tallied the days: two weeks now. They had no trail to follow, but Caine was confident he could find a lead somewhere. Ask a few questions, keep your ears open, and you'll pick up word of a man traveling with a boy, he assured them. He and Orion had ridden out of sight across the hills, generally following the southward course of the Rio Bravo. Seahorn will go south, Caine had said, down into the hilly, empty Big Bend country where a man can hide, and where he can find his friend Old Pablo, whoever that might be.

Brice had wept in frustration when they left, but he tried to hide it, so Rosalita pretended not to notice, even though she would have liked to comfort him. Now he did not weep. He merely stared out the window, said almost nothing, ate almost nothing.

The worst part was that now he could barely move his legs. Whether it was a delayed effect of the bullet he had taken in Serveto, or some blunder of the amateurish medical man Ria had brought in to dig out the slug, they did not know. All they knew was that after the slug came out, Brice had lost most of the movement and feeling from the waist down. The so-called doctor muttered apologies, waived his fee, and rode away. He took for a souvenir the bullet he had not too gently dug out.

Rosalita went back to Brice's door. He still sat as before, just staring.

"You want coffee?"

Nothing.

"Water, then? Or I will go to town and bring you beer if you wish."

"Just leave me alone," he said, and the way he said it hurt. She withdrew, closing the door after her.

Brice tried again to move his feet, and he could not.

Though he had spent all his life in Texas, Keelan had never before seen a dust storm like the one that loomed before them now. It was as if some superhuman painter had dipped a broad brush in too-dry pigment of dirty orange and roughly slapped it across the sky. Except in this painting the smear of color was moving, almost writhing, rolling across the desert like a hoop snake.

As he had since they had left Serveto, Neal Seahorn turned in the saddle and looked behind him. Again and again, and each time seeming concerned, maybe even scared.

He looked that way all the time now, Keelan noted. Sometimes in the night Seahorn would start upright, breath whooshing out and eyes wide, as if he was looking back into a nightmare. "Alianza," he would say. "Alianza." And then settle back to sleep with Keelan's wrist tied to his.

Now Seahorn watched the dust storm, about a mile away from them, and smiled. "That'll hide our trail well enough," he said. "Let them find me through that!" He turned and looked behind them again.

Keelan looked, too. "There's nobody there," he said.

"Alianza is there, boy. Alianza is everywhere you look."

Seahorn pulled his bandana across his face. He reached into his vest pocket and pulled out another, which he gave to Keelan. The kerchief smelled like sweat and cigarette smoke, but Keelan tied it across his face anyway, for he knew how a dust storm could choke a person.

"They'll never find us now," Seahorn said again as they moved forward into the storm.

It seemed to roll down to meet them. Stinging pieces of sand and grit against the skin, burning the eyes, making the hair feel like a skullcap of dirt on Keelan's head. He hunched over his saddlehorn, squinting, suffering under the buffeting. Seahorn's shoulders were pulled up to hug his neck, and he rode low in the saddle, but Keelan could tell he didn't mind the storm. Maybe even was enjoying it. Keelan wondered if Seahorn was crazy.

Distance was almost impossible to calculate in this hell of wind and sand, direction even more so. Yet Seahorn seemed determined to continue. The storm did not abate.

At length Seahorn stopped; Keelan did the same. Seahorn pointed wordlessly at a little house of adobe, alternately visible and invisible through the storm. One moment it was stark and clear, the next invisible as a ghost place when the wind kicked up more dust.

"Come on, boy."

Keelan dutifully put his heels into the flanks of his wind-tortured horse. They rode slowly toward the house. A little shed came into view through the dust storm, and

Seahorn motioned for Keelan to follow him there. Once inside, Keelan pulled down the foul-smelling bandana, coughed, and spit out sand, then took a deep breath of fetid air. Sand blew in through cracks in the wall.

A nearly starved burro stood in a stall nearby. There was water in a wooden bucket for it, and Seahorn took some and gave it to the horses.

"Shouldn't we ask?" Keelan suggested, then realized how foolish that must sound to Seahorn.

"Come with me, boy," Seahorn said to him. He pushed open the door and they went out into the storm.

It seemed to take forever to trudge to the house. Keelan expected Seahorn to knock, but he didn't. Instead he just pushed open the door and walked in.

An old man was inside. His eyes were strange, looking in the wrong direction. He pulled back fearfully at the sound of the door; in Spanish he asked who was there.

"Just some dust-bit riders, old man," Seahorn said. "You speak the English, Mex?"

"Sí, some English, some English. Please do not shoot me. Blind. I am blind."

Seahorn was patting dust off his clothes. He stopped, leaned over, and looked into the man's face.

"Be damned—so you are," he said. "You got any food, old man?"

"Little food, señor. My son, he is gone for many days, working to north. He was to come back but he has not."

"Why, he might be dead, old man," Seahorn said, laughing. "You might just starve like a rat out here in the middle of these godforsaken badlands."

He began stalking about the little house, looking in boxes, on the table. "Haven't you got anything but tortillas, old man?" he said. "Look at that—covered with ants—not fit to eat."

Keelan approached the old man. The blind eyes were a filmy blue, cocked at a strange angle. "I'm sorry," Keelan whispered as Seahorn continued to thrash about. "He is a bad man."

"You are only a *muchacho*!" the old man whispered.

"Yes. I don't steal. He steals."

The old man's voice dropped to a whisper. "You are, you are..." He was struggling for the right word. "You are—kidnapped?"

"Yes. How did you—"

"Much talk for a long time—ones who pass talk of a boy kidnapped many days ago in Kensington—"

"Shut up in there," Seahorn barked. "Get away from him, boy."

Keelan drew away. He had a peculiar feeling, though, that the old man was looking at him with those blind eyes, trying to tell him something. The man's head was twitching in an unnatural way, as if he were trying to shake a fly off his nose without using his hands. Suddenly Keelan understood: the old man was gesturing to his right. Keelan looked.

An old rifle, its stock thrusting out from under a cloth-draped table. Keelan's mouth went dry. He felt frozen in his place.

Seahorn stomped back in and went to the door. He opened it and peered out. Wind howled in, blowing in grit. Seahorn drew his pistol.

"They're out there," he said.

"Who?" Keelan asked.

"Alianza, you little jackass!" Seahorn thrust his pistol out the door and fired. The report made the old man start and moan. The blind eyes rolled in their sockets.

Seahorn fired again, then cursed as if he had missed. Keelan went to a window and peeped out through a cracked shutter.

"There's nobody there," he said, and there wasn't. Nothing but blowing dust and sand, and the far-stretching barrens.

"I can see them. I can even smell them. Everywhere I go they follow me."

He really is crazy, Keelan thought. Keelan had heard vague scraps of talk around the dinner table about the Alianza, and he had gathered that it was something most people, his grandfather included, didn't even believe existed. He had heard the word mentioned by his guards in Serveto but still had only an imprecise notion about what it might be.

Whatever it was, though, Seahorn certainly believed in it and was scared of it. So scared he saw it where there was nothing.

I've got to get away from him, Keelan thought. *He's crazy enough that sooner or later he'll just get tired of dragging me along and kill me.* The thought made Keelan's empty stomach knot up like a wad of wet twine. He looked once more at the old man's hidden rifle.

An old musket of some kind. Something out of Civil War times, maybe, or even before. Keelan glanced again at Seahorn, who was still peering through the storm at his imaginary enemies.

The stock of the rifle seemed to attract Keelan's eyes, magnetlike. The old man was rolling his head again, obviously trying to get Keelan to pick up the weapon.

Keelan swallowed and went half a step toward it. He watched Seahorn, edged a little closer, a little more. Seahorn did not turn.

Keelan suddenly was afraid he would cry. He bit his lip and forced back the tears that brimmed in his eyes. Could he even aim a weapon at a living man, much less squeeze the trigger?

I've got to, he thought. *Else he'll kill me, leave me dead out there for the buzzards.*

In one sweeping motion he reached the rifle and drew it out. The old man heard the motion, smiled. The hoary old head with its unseeing eyes bobbed up and down.

Keelan was shaking as he raised the old cap-and-ball rifle. He prayed that the rifle was loaded and at the same time half-hoped it was not. It seemed to weigh a hundred pounds as he leveled it, aimed it—

For what seemed a much longer time than it really was he stood there, holding up the heavy old rifle, trying to stop the muzzle from waving back and forth as he homed it in on Seahorn.

Seahorn raised his pistol and fired into the storm again just as Keelan numbly squeezed the trigger of the rifle. The hammer fell on a dead cap, the snap of it masked by Seahorn's pistol blast. Keelan felt tears erupt. He slid the useless rifle back into its place. The tears would not stop, and now he was starting to blubber. He sank to the floor, trembling and hiding his face behind his upraised knees. The old man's head was still bobbing, but now he was praying to the Virgin, a weird chanting that sounded like an Indian deathsong.

Seahorn suddenly laughed. Keelan choked off his tears by sheer will, wiped his eyes, and looked up. Seahorn was holstering the pistol.

"Why, there wasn't anybody there to begin with!" he said. "Imagine that! Just shapes in the dust."

I wish I could go find my father and be home again and never, never leave, Keelan thought.

Chapter 18

It was a little community where trails crossed—a half-dozen adobe houses like squat boxes on the land, a round well with a block wall, a stable with a horse cuartel, a general store, a blacksmithy, and a cantina. The name of this smattering of buildings they did not even know. Here Simon Caine and Orion Jones rode as the sun edged down on the hills and made the sky look like ruby.

A few miles westward the Rio Bravo flowed slow as syrup, unhurriedly moving south toward the rugged place where it would bend east and then northeast. Before reaching there it would run in a speeding torrent through three canyons and past some of the most rugged and inhospitable country in all of Texas. It was in that country, Caine believed, that he would find Seahorn and young Keelan. With any luck, he would learn something in this cantina that might help him toward that end.

Caine's eyes swept over Orion as he dismounted. It struck him that in the brief time he had known the young man, he had become more hardened. The gaze of his black eyes was more flinty and piercing than before. Orion could have been an offspring of the very barren landscape through which they traveled. This life was transforming him.

"You getting down?" he asked Orion.

Orion rested his right hand on the stock of the booted revolving Colt rifle and shook his head. "Don't feel very comfortable here, somehow."

"Suit yourself. I'll bring you a bottle."

"I don't drink."

"A man with no vices is hard to be nice to, Orion."

There were only three men inside the cantina. All three quit talking and openly stared at Caine when he entered. One of them rose and went to the other side of the homemade bar.

"You got beer? *Cerveza?*"

"*Sí.* Good beer, but hot."

"I'll take what I can get. And buy some for my friends, here."

That brought smiles. The two other men rose and came to the bar to accept their unexpected gift. One was an Anglo, the other a Mexican who looked as if he might have some Apache or Comanche blood mixed in.

"*Gracias,*" said the half-breed. The Anglo said thanks in English with a flat Texas accent.

"Been riding far, *amigo?*" the Anglo asked.

"Far enough," Caine said. "Looking for somebody. Maybe you've seen him."

"Maybe. Who?"

"Fellow about my age, maybe a couple years older. Riding with a boy maybe ten or eleven."

Something changed in the look and stance of all three men. The barkeep turned away and busied himself wiping out his kiln-fired beer mugs with a towel. The half-breed took a long swallow and looked at Caine out of the corner of his eye, and the Anglo coughed unconvincingly a couple of times and took some gulps of beer as if to settle his throat. He backhanded foam off his mouth.

"Man and a boy... let's see. Nope. Don't recall seeing any such."

Caine smiled. "I see. When was it you didn't see him?"

For a moment the Anglo took offense at the delicate sarcasm, but his half-breed partner laughed and that softened him. He smiled.

"No offense, mister, but I like to know why a question is being asked before I answer it."

"Easy enough. The man stole that boy away from his kin. I want to get him back."

"You his pappy?"

"Uncle."

The Anglo took another swallow and looked as if he was thinking something over. Finally he gave a quick, resolute nod.

"All right, I'll level with you. I did see him, maybe a day, day and a half ago. Right here. Seemed nervous, looked behind him a lot." The man paused before he added, "And he looked a heck of a lot like Neal Seahorn to me."

"So he is."

"And you're tracking him? Seahorn's not to be fooled with, I hear tell."

"He fooled with me first."

The half-breed laughed again and spoke for the first time. "You are a confident man, *señor.*"

"Just concerned about my nephew. Which way were they heading?"

"South. He didn't say, but I'd guess he's bound for the Chisos Mountains. If you're hiding, that's the place to go."

"He buy anything?"

"A couple of water bags and a canteen. A little liquor, a new bridle. Had his horses reshod. Bought some flour and such at the store."

"So he had money."

"Biggest wad I ever seen. Lord, why am I talking so free? He comes back through, he might plug me if it gets out I blabbed on him."

"He won't come back through."

The half-breed said, "Who is the buck outside with the rifle?"

Caine glanced up in the bar mirror. In its reflection of the street outside the open door he saw Orion still tensely mounted. He had drawn the Colt rifle.

"Friend of mine," Caine said.

"What a rifle! Made like a pistol."

"Yeah. What's in the Chisos Mountains?"

"Mostly jackrabbits, turkey vultures, scorpions, and your occasional bandido. You may have trouble finding him once he gets there."

"I'll find him." Caine drained his mug. "Obliged, gentlemen."

"Not meaning to be forward, but what's your name?"

Caine smiled and touched his hat. He walked out the door without another word. The two men came after him and stood in the doorway, watching. Orion stared back at them nervously.

"You look jumpy as a hot frog," Caine said to Orion as he untethered.

"I don't like it here. Let's go."

"Hold your horses. Where we're going we're going to need more supplies."

Orion looked displeased. He nudged heels into horse flanks and moved to the center of the dusty street. Caine led his horse to the general store that stood diagonally across from the cantina and retethered there. Orion rode farther down and then held up at the end of the street, sitting mounted with his rifle butt parked on his hip. Caine frowned. To any casual observer who did not know him, Orion would look as if he were pondering gunning down the entire populace—something he could probably do in this tiny place with only one reload, Caine noted. Caine determined to give Orion some lessons at first opportunity in how to be inconspicuous.

Caine had little money, so he tried to spend it wisely. Brice had carried this cash hidden in his boot and had not lost it at Serveto. Caine bought jerked meat, flour, hard biscuits, coffee, some extra ammunition, and other supplies. He walked out laden with goods, trying to figure how best to divide the load between their horses. Then he stopped cold.

Two men were talking to Orion, and Orion looked none too happy about it. Caine glanced at the cantina; the half-breed Mex-Indian guiltily slipped back into the interior darkness just as Caine saw him. Caine remembered the 'breed's question about Orion and realized there might have been more behind it than idle curiosity. The half-breed might have sent out some kind of alert while Caine was occupied in the store.

Trying to look casual, Caine untied his horse and walked steadily toward Orion, leading the horse and carrying the supplies at the same time. Orion shot a disturbing glance at him that let Caine know the situation could quickly get out of control. *Take it easy, Orion. Be calm*, Caine mentally commanded.

"Howdy, gentlemen," Caine said. "Pretty day."

One said hello and the other nodded. "I'm Dorthal Abernathy," the first said. "I'm sort of a constable here, you know. Just talking to your partner for a minute."

Caine smiled. "He's careless about flashing that rifle. You'll do better, won't you, Fred? Sure you will."

"Fred?" Dorthal Abernathy swung his skinny frame toward Orion. "You said your name was Orion."

Caine winced inwardly and added how to lie to Orion's list of overdue lessons.

Orion looked at Caine in wild-eyed helplessness. Caine shrugged.

Suddenly Abernathy had a big Dragoon pistol leveled on Orion. His partner, an equally skinny man whom Caine suddenly realized might well be Abernathy's son, had Caine staring into the black eye of a cut-down Winchester rifle with a sawed-off stock.

"There's reports of a young nigger buck with a revolving rifle killing a white man up at Kensington," Abernathy announced. To Caine he said, "Don't know just who you are, mister, but you're both coming with us."

"Pa . . ."

"What, boy?"

"We ain't got no jail."

Under other circumstances Caine would have laughed at the way Abernathy's eyes widened at that comment. Abernathy stood there with his mouth steadily drawing up like a sphincter.

Orion quietly leveled the revolving Colt and thumbed back the hammer. Abernathy swallowed. The Colt rifle shook as Orion trembled.

Caine turned to Abernathy's son. "You don't want your daddy to get hurt, do you?"

The young man shook his head.

"Put down that chopped-off rifle, then."

Abernathy, meanwhile, still had his Colt Dragoon leveled on Orion. The two men looked at each other in a hopeless standoff.

The younger Abernathy stooped and laid his unusual weapon on the street. Dorthal Abernathy harked up and spat in disgust, then lowered his Dragoon. He handed it to Caine.

"Never wanted to be constable no how," he said.

"Mister, I've seen places do a lot worse for law officers with grit," Caine said as he took the Dragoon. He also picked up the sawed-off rifle. "I'll leave these on the ground about a mile south. And if you'll excuse us now, gentlemen, we've got to go kill Neal Seahorn."

Orion had little to say for a long time after they rode out. Night spread its ink over the sky, and they made camp under a large basalt escarpment whose black upright plane surface blended up into the dark sky as if it had no end.

Orion unloaded the Colt rifle and carefully began cleaning it in the light of the small fire they allowed themselves. They built it near the escarpment base, piling stones around it some distance away to help hide its glow from any direction.

"Where did you get that revolving rifle?" Caine asked.

"My pa's. Don't rightly know where he got it." Orion lifted his eyes for a moment. "I think maybe it was stole."

"Oh."

"Pa said these rifles come out in '57. Mr. Sam Colt made them for a regiment up in Connecticut that they named after him. They busted up in '61, and all the rifles was supposed to go back to the armory."

"But not all of them did."

Orion smiled. "This one didn't, at least. But I really don't know how Pa got it. He sure wasn't in no Sam Colt regiment during the war."

"Pretty gun. Takes a .44?"

"Yeah. But I'll have to get myself something newer and better soon."

Caine understood. "You're on the run."

Orion nodded. "You heard what they said back there. They're looking for me."

"Did you really kill somebody?"

"Sure did. Didn't really mean to. A man who worked on the ranch—he's the one who told Seahorn's kidnappers where to get Keelan and my pa."

Caine had been making coffee, and now he took the pot off the fire. He poured a cupful for Orion, then for himself. "I know what it means to lose kin to killers," he said.

"If I can get vengeance, I'll be all right," Orion said.

Caine took a swallow of the scalding black coffee. "Don't throw away your life for the likes of Seahorn."

"How can you say that? What about all you did? Robert Montrose and all that?"

Caine had no answer.

Orion rubbed an oily cloth over his rifle's cylinder, working silently for several minutes. "How you reckon Mr. Brice is doing?" he finally said.

"Well, I hope. If he dies—"

"He won't die, Mr. Caine. And you just wait—he'll walk again. I'll bet he is already."

But Brice wasn't walking. In fact, it was a struggle for him even to stand. He could drag himself along with great effort, but rarely could he take a real step. Usually it was more like heaving one rag-doll leg forward, locking the knee, vaulting over, heaving the other leg, locking the knee, doing the same. All the while clutching the bedpost or leaning against the wall.

Brice had long ago overcome the self-pity he had felt after the wartime injury that had left him with a permanent limp. A limp, after all, could be lived with. A man didn't have to walk smoothly to get around.

But this, he thought as he lay awake tonight—this was much worse. He was a cripple. Just like Garth Kensington had been just before he—

Brice realized he had just thought of Kensington as dead. And dead he probably was, judging from the shape he had been in when Brice left. Maybe that was for the best. It was likely, after all, that Keelan would never come home. Seahorn would kill him out there somewhere. Likely they would never even find the body. Keelan would be dead, Garth would be dead, and Brice himself a cripple—

Brice pushed himself up in his bed. No! He would not surrender hope for Keelan, not until he knew certainly that he was dead. Nor would he quit trying to walk.

He threw his legs over the edge of the bed. He wiggled his toes—at least he could do that. His spine was injured, not broken.

Closing his eyes, he took a deep breath, then pushed himself to his feet. He wavered, reached for the bedpost to steady himself. He wiggled his toes again—and felt it, though his legs still seemed wooden and detached.

Here goes, he thought.

In her own bed in the next room, Rosalita heard the sound of his collapse. She bolted up and in her gown rushed to Brice's room. He lay just inside the door, facedown.

"Brice—"

She knelt beside him as he rolled over. He took her hand and squeezed it. He was smiling broadly.

"Six steps. Six steps before I fell."

He put his arms around her neck, drew her down, and kissed her.

Chapter 19

"There they are, boy," Neal Seahorn said as he pointed.

Keelan was already looking. Ahead, rising from the sprawling desert floor, stood a hazy line of volcanic mountains. Their contrast to the red-brown landscape was remarkable; for along the mountain crests were green forests of madrone, pine, and juniper. These were the Chisos Mountains, which seemed to grow from the parched Chihuahuan Desert like some hardy plant.

"A man can get himself swallowed up down there," Seahorn said with satisfaction. "That's just what we're going to do, boy." He gave another habitual glance over his shoulder, then spurred his tired mount forward. Keelan's own horse also lurched into step again, its head low with weariness.

Keelan rode with his wrists bound together and roped to the saddlehorn. The ropes were too tight and burned him, but he did not ask Seahorn to loosen them. The last time he had asked, Seahorn had sworn at him and pulled them tighter.

The closer they drew to the mountains the more the desert became a place of life. Keelan saw two roadrunners dart among the scrubby desert brush. Mice scampered, hawks circled, a jackrabbit watched them from a safe distance before loping off, and scorpions vanished off rocks like bugs escaping a newly fired stove.

Vultures circling overhead lent an ominous cast to the area, but even Keelan couldn't miss the beauty into which they were riding. But he dreaded going farther into it. He had no idea what would become of him once they were hidden in the mountains. His father, whom he had never doubted was searching for him, might never find him in the Chisos. Eventually Seahorn might tire of having a boy along, even a boy who could potentially bring him a big ransom, and what would happen then?

Keelan quietly tugged at his ropes. He had to find a way to escape.

Noon waned into afternoon, but the heat remained intense. Such was the way of the desert: reflecting back intense and unfiltered sun rays all day, making the desert floor hot as a skillet, then casting off all its accumulated heat at night until land and atmosphere were almost bitterly cold.

Ravines began marking the land, deep ruts that led to the Rio Bravo to the west. The vegetation here was almost exclusively thorny mesquite. They pushed on.

At last the trail began to rise; they reached a high point and then descended into a gulch filled with juniper and piñon. The north slopes of the Chisos range stood uplifted before them, their sheer volcanic walls defying penetration. Into the gulch they descended, leaving the true desert behind. They reached at length a wide depression particularly rich in vegetation, including madrone, oak, ponderosa pine, even quaking aspen. Night was nearly upon them now, and Seahorn halted. "We'll sleep here," he said. He said it reluctantly; Keelan could tell Seahorn wanted to push on into the mountains.

"Where are we going?" Keelan asked.

Seahorn smiled. "Old Pablo lives yonder. He'll put us up where even Alianza won't find us."

They ate a meager hardtack supper and lay down. The horses grazed on the wild grasses and drank at a little seep into which Seahorn had dug a water collection trench.

Keelan did not go to sleep as quickly as usual even though he was very tired. His thoughts ran like a runaway wagon; he had a strong notion that his time with Seahorn was approaching an end—one way or another. *Well, if that is to be it, then let the end be tomorrow,* he thought. *Whatever happens, and however it happens, the end of this will be tomorrow.*

Seahorn kicked Keelan awake the next morning. "Come on," he barked. "We're going to Old Pablo's place."

"I'm hungry."

"Pablo will have grub."

Seahorn busied himself tensely. Still he looked around and back constantly, searching for the Alianza pursuers who were, in his mind at least, always just behind. But today he also bubbled with seeming anticipation. Keelan realized that Seahorn saw this Old Pablo's place, wherever and whatever that was, as a sanctuary where he would at last be safe. It gave Keelan an uneasy feeling. He remembered his mental pledge, *Today, somehow, I will be free of him.*

They mounted. Seahorn tied Keelan again. They rode through bigtooth maples and beneath red cliffs, until the land finally began transforming back to something more resembling desert. They crossed a sand wash and picked their way through long stretches of creosote, ocotillo, and cacti. The day stretched itself awake after the cool night; the sun grew hotter and more intense, flaring like a blacksmith's bellow-fed fire. The night had been characterized by the buzzing singsong of insects, but that gave way to stillness. The desert became quiet except for the sound of the wind, of their horses plodding along, of Seahorn whistling a tune Keelan did not know.

They rode for a long time, stopping occasionally to water themselves and the horses and to rest in whatever shade they could find. During those times Seahorn would first sit a few moments, then rise and scan the horizon, sit again. Over and over. Keelan had been brave throughout his whole ordeal, but now his courage began to waver. It was hard to keep back tears. He began to think that the only way he would escape today would be through death whenever they reached this Old Pablo's place that Seahorn apparently regarded as his mecca.

But Keelan did not cry. After each stop they remounted, Seahorn tied Keelan again, and they rode on. At last they came to a canyon about four hundred feet deep and descended into its limestone depths. The horses moved eagerly, with new energy, for they smelled water below.

The floor of the canyon featured numerous tinajas, or natural water tanks. They rode to the nearest one, frightening off an array of birds, a rattlesnake, and a porcine-looking javelina. Seahorn filled their canteens and water bags as the horses drank. Here at the base of the canyon it was much more cool than above. Also darker, the undulatory walls casting deep shade.

Seahorn slapped a mosquito on his neck and wiped it on his trousers leg. "Old Pablo's isn't far now," he said. He almost sounded friendly, even fatherly. It made Keelan despise him all the more.

The boy asked, "When will you let me go home?"

"This is no time to think of that," Seahorn returned.

After the horses were grazed and watered, they rode on. The sun dipped toward the west. Keelan realized they hadn't eaten all day, not even during their stops. Yet he wasn't hungry; the sense of dread that had ridden on his shoulders all day kept him from it.

After another hour the noticeably excited Seahorn stopped and pointed up a ridge. "There it is, boy!" he said. "Pablo! Hey, Pablo! It's Neal!"

Keelan had to squint to make out the rough stone wall built onto a wide ledge up the ridge. The spot apparently was inaccessible but for a steep dry wash that cut into the side of the slope. A rider could pass this place and never know it was there. The dark door and two windows that seemed to peer down at them blended into the natural colors of the stone.

"Pablo!" Seahorn shouted again. No sound in response.

Their tired horses labored up the wash, their hooves kicking down avalanches of gravel. Finally they reached the ledge and stopped. Seahorn dismounted.

"Pablo?"

He edged forward, toward the door. Keelan saw now that this dwelling was merely a front stone wall built over a natural deep depression in the slope.

Seahorn's heart hammered. Something was wrong here

and he could feel it. He slipped silently to the door, then went inside. No one there.

"Pablo?"

A half-filled lamp lay on its side on a table made from a stone slab: Seahorn sat up the lamp and lit it. He lifted it and looked around the room.

"No, Pablo. No . . ."

The old man apparently had died months ago, for bones were all that remained of him. most of them lay about the back of the dwelling and others were scattered all across the room—probably by coyotes. From beneath a stool Pablo's skull, still retaining a few tufts of hair and bits of leathery skin, peered back at Seahorn, the toothless jaw open.

Seahorn turned and sadly walked outside again.

It took him a moment to notice that Keelan was gone. The boy had slipped his ropes and run away on foot.

Keelan ran scared, not well. He left a clear trail, and most of the time he stayed in the open. The farther he got from Seahorn the more sure he felt that he had done the wrong thing. Seahorn would quickly track him down and kill him.

Keelan hadn't even thought to take one of the canteens with him, nor any food. But none of that could matter now—he must run as hard and far as he could.

By the time Keelan stopped, he had gone more than a mile. He was exhausted and collapsed in a shaded arroyo, panting.

Simon Caine knelt by a tinaja and studied marks in the wet sand. "They were here, all right," he said to Orion, who was still mounted. "And not only them—there's tracks of another rider."

"Another rider? Who would that be?"

"Don't know. But it appears whoever it is, he's tracking Seahorn just like we are."

Orion dismounted and studied the marks. He was not the tracker Caine was, but even he could see that Caine was right.

"You think the Alianza has somebody following Seahorn?" Orion asked.

"Don't know. Anything's possible. Whatever, we're going to have to look sharp. If we know about him, he may know about us."

"But why haven't we spotted these tracks before now?"

"I have, but never clear. I didn't want to say anything until I was sure."

Caine mounted, and he and Orion rode for another hour deeper into the rugged country. Wind rustled through the acacias; somewhere an owl hooted. The air began to grow cool and the light dimmer.

"Going to have to give it up for tonight," Caine said.

Orion nodded. "Too bad. I was hoping we'd—"

The bullet struck a moment before the sound reached them. Chips of blue-gray stone exploded from a boulder against which Orion had been outlined. He reacted instantly— bent low over his saddlehorn, spurred his mount forward and into a cluster of brush growing around a seep.

Caine, meanwhile, cut to the right, gracefully leaped from his saddle when his horse was safely behind a wall-like limestone face, and freed his rifle from the saddle boot. He scanned the upper lines of the ridges, searching for some movement against the rich, blue-black sky.

Another shot, and this one almost hit Caine. He saw where it had come from—lower on the ridge, maybe from a ledge. Caine strained his eyes in the growing dark. He thought he made out the outline of the door, maybe windows, against the cambered ridge. Some kind of dwelling built up there—and occupied by somebody with an unfriendly way of welcome.

"Who are you?" The voice echoed down from above. "Why have you been following me?"

Orion whisper-shouted to Caine, "That Seahorn?"

"Yep," Caine returned.

Another blast of fire; Caine pinpointed this one even more exactly. He lined up his sites.

"Who are you? Are you Alianza?" Seahorn yelled.

Caine shouted back. "The boy, Neal. Give him to me."

A long pause. "Simon? How the devil..." Another pause, then another shot. This time Caine fired back.

"There's two of us to one of you, Neal," he shouted. "Let's talk. All I want is the boy."

"Why? What's he to you?"

"My nephew, Neal. Believe that or not. But I want him."

He heard a strange vocal sound echo down: Seahorn's laugh, distorted as it bounced down between the facing ridges. "Well, Simon, you can't have him! Couldn't give him to you if I wanted, now!"

Orion said, "That must mean he's dead, Simon."

Caine gritted his teeth; a deep rage surged inside him and geysered out. "You're a dead man, Neal!" he shouted.

Caine moved out from behind the stone face and darted along the edge of a tinaja. Two shots from above sent bullets into the water. Caine leaped from one side of the natural water tank to another, rolled, and came up firing. He apparently got close enough to worry Seahorn; no gunfire came in response for several seconds.

"Simon! What are you doing?" Orion shouted. When Caine didn't answer, Orion came out after him.

Now Seahorn fired repeatedly again, almost hitting Orion three times. Orion slipped and fell into the tinaja; his rifle dropped from his grip and sank to the bottom of the tank.

Caine backtracked and extended his hand to Orion. Above he heard Seahorn laugh, then Seahorn fired again and Orion grunted and fell. The water turned pink around him.

Caine yelled and reached again for Orion. The black man struggled to his feet, gripping a bleeding shoulder.

"Give me your good hand!" Caine shouted. Orion did, reaching out with gory fingers. Hands clasped, Caine heaved back, and Orion was almost out of the tinaja when another slug tore through him and jolted him back in.

Caine dropped his rifle and went in after Orion. He dragged the limp form out, hefted him across his shoulder, and carried him to cover as Seahorn laughed and fired from above. Amazingly, Caine made it. Then he ran back to where his rifle lay, picked it up, and found meager cover behind a pile of stones.

Caine looked up, and now in the last light of the day he saw Seahorn. The man had recklessly exposed himself at the edge of the bluff.

Caine lifted his rifle, got Seahorn in the sights.

"Where's the boy?" he shouted.

Seahorn laughed again. "He's gone, Simon. Got loose and ran away. What, you thought I'd killed him?"

Suddenly Seahorn moved back, firing carelessly down as he did so. Caine lowered his rifle.

"Keelan! If you're there, let me hear you!" Caine shouted. Nothing in response but Seahorn's laugh, more muffled than before, for Seahorn had gone back inside Old Pablo's cliffside dwelling.

"Keelan? Are you there?"

Still nothing.

Caine reached inside his jacket and drew out two sticks of dynamite wrapped in canvas. He loosened the canvas's ties, then used them to bind the sticks together. He intertwined the fuses.

Something moved above. Seahorn fired down again. He missed Caine, but not by much.

"I know Alianza sent you, Simon!" he shouted. "Don't tell me different!"

"I don't work for the Alianza—you know that," Caine shouted back as he struck a match on the rocks and lit the fuses. "This is a family matter, Neal."

The long fuses burned steadily down toward the deadly sticks in Caine's hand. "I got ransom for you, Neal!" Caine yelled. "I'm sending it up!"

He stood and threw the dynamite. It was almost dark now, and the fuses made a sparkling line as they arced up. Caine's aim was true, but he had miscalculated by a second the burn time of the fuses. The twin explosions came just before the sticks would have landed in the doorway of the house of Old Pablo.

The blast illuminated the night as it blew in the wall with incredible force, throwing stones back into the interior as if shot from cannons.

A few minutes later, when Caine had found Seahorn

amid the rubble, the dying man looked at him and said, "Simon . . . you swear to me that Alianza didn't send you?"

"I swear it, Neal. I came on my own, for the boy. If I had wanted to work for the Alianza, I'd have taken you up on your offer in Serveto."

Seahorn smiled. "So, Alianza didn't get me after all. Looks like the joke's on them."

"Looks like it."

Seahorn closed his eyes. "Never wanted to let those bluebellies through at Murfreesboro, Simon. I'm mighty sorry."

"We made it out all right."

"I'm tired. I want to rest."

"You do that, Neal."

Seahorn nodded. His breathing deepened and became steady, and then it stopped. Simon Caine laid the body down and crawled back out over the rubble.

Chapter 20

Caine gave a final check to Orion's bandages and said, "You're going to be fine, son. You were lucky you got hit no worse than you did."

"It don't feel lucky," Orion said. "It hurts."

"We need to sleep now. Come first light I'll be leaving you here so I can look for Keelan."

The sunrise was clear the next morning; the day would be one of those searingly bright ones the desert often served up. As Caine saddled his horse, he worried over Keelan. He hardly knew the boy despite his kinship; Keelan, indeed, had no idea that Caine was his uncle. Still, Caine found his concern for Keelan was hardly less than that he would have felt for his own son in such a predicament.

"I won't be gone too long, Orion," Caine said. "Keelan probably didn't get far, and besides, I can't just run out on you with you shot up."

"I'll make it fine. You find the boy," Orion said.

Caine had no idea at what point Keelan had escaped Seahorn, nor which direction he would have taken, so he decided to trust his instinct and his own memories of how the mind of a boy works. Keelan, he figured, had probably tried to put as much distance as possible between himself and Seahorn, meaning he probably kept mostly in the clear when running away. But he might have taken to the rocks, too, to find a place to hide.

Caine followed the most obvious route through the rugged terrain, gambling on the chance Keelan in his haste had done the same. At last he came to a place requiring a turn either south or north, and there he stopped and dismounted. Slowly and carefully he studied the earth all about, and at last found what he thought might be a portion of a boy-sized footprint. He went in the direction it indicated, passed over an expanse of bare gray rock, then beyond that found another footprint, this one deeper and more obvious. Caine nodded—he was on the right track.

He returned to his mount and rode along the path Keelan had followed, but eventually the route sloped up and he had to lead his horse. Finally even that became difficult, and he looked for a place to hobble his mount while he continued on alone.

He saw a narrow passage between two rocks, and beyond it a little natural cove filled with grass. A good place for his horse, if he could get it through the small opening. He tried and succeeded, but once inside, stopped and stared.

Another horse already was here, grazing. It had a saddle on its back.

Something moved above. Caine turned, drawing his pistol. He saw nothing but almost mentally detected a presence behind a line of rocks above the enclave. It seemed for a moment that he also heard a muffled exclamation of some sort—the voice of a boy.

"Keelan?" Caine said. "That you?"

Movement at another place now. Caine turned again, looking up. He was facing east and had to stare almost directly into the sun to see the figure that rose above him on the rim of the rocks enclosing this place. Sun-blinded, he could make out no details, but the figure was too large to be Keelan. Then he saw a smaller form beside the larger one.

"Keelan? You all right?"

"For now," the man with the boy said. "Hello, Caine. I've been waiting a long time to meet you."

Caine still held his pistol. "Who are you?"

"My name is Morrison Deguere. Perhaps you've heard of me."

"Afraid not."

"Strange. Like you. I've got something of a reputation. I've also got your young friend."

Caine moved slightly to his left to get a better view. He could ascertain a bit about Deguere's looks now—rather long beard, derby on the head, and clothing that looked too heavy for this clime. "I want the boy safe," Caine said.

"Certainly. For a price."

"What are you talking about?"

"First, drop the pistol, then kick it away. It makes me nervous." Deguere moved a bit and Caine saw he held a gun on Keelan's neck. "Drop it or I will have to do something unfortunate to your nephew here."

Keelan frowned, confused by Deguere's reference to him as a nephew of the man whose voice he recognized as that of the occupant of the cell adjacent to his in Serveto. For Caine's part, he could do nothing but comply. He dropped the pistol and toed it away.

"Very good, Caine. Let me tell you something about myself. I am a detective and I work for William Montrose. He is paying me quite well to see you dead, and though you don't know it, I've trailed you since you left the Bitterroots. More recently I've been trailing Neal Seahorn and this young man instead, ever since they left Serveto. You see, my goal is to gain whatever money I can, however I can get it, and I figured Seahorn to have a lot of it. I was surprised, I admit, to find the boy wandering alone out here. He tells me he evaded Seahorn."

Caine said, "If Montrose wants me, take me. Let Keelan go."

"Oh, no. He's a good source of insurance—I know you'll try nothing as long as I've got him. But tell me, Caine, where is Seahorn?"

"Looking for his lost hostage, I figure. Probably drawing a bead on you right now." Caine lied without missing a beat.

Deguere laughed. "I can see you're still a conniver, Caine. I'll get no straight talk from you. I'm coming down with the boy now. You move and he's dead. Now I'm going to—"

Neither Deguere nor Caine anticipated Keelan's next

move. With a quick, catlike twist he pulled away from Deguere's grasp, then elbowed Deguere in the crotch. The man's eyes bulged, his breath burst out, and he doubled over. Keelan scrambled away, and Caine made a dive for his pistol.

Deguere roared and fired a shot in anger at Keelan, but the boy darted behind some rocks and it missed. Then Deguere remembered Caine and trained his pistol down on him. Caine reached his own pistol and fired just as Deguere also did. Neither man hit his target. But Deguere knew better than to wait for Caine to have a second shot, so he backstepped away from the edge of the bluff and Caine's potential line of fire.

Caine exited the rocky enclave as fast as he could, then cut back to the left and up a wash. He searched for both Keelan and Deguere but saw neither. Suddenly something exploded behind him and a bullet struck the earth at his feet. He overreacted and fell, rolling back several feet down the wash. He heard Deguere laugh, then another shot. At first he was amazed that this one, too, had missed, but then he saw blood and realized he had been grazed in the calf.

He made it up the wash and came out on the same rocky area on which Deguere had stood earlier when he still had Keelan prisoner. Caine heard motion behind him, turned, and caught a glimpse of Deguere moving from behind one boulder to another. Between the two Deguere fired, almost hitting Caine in the face. Caine tried to fire back but found his pistol had become jammed as he scrambled up the wash.

He ran, trying to fix the weapon at the same time, but it was no use. After Seahorn had been killed, Caine had stashed his other pistol in a saddlebag, figuring he would not need it. He now wished he had it.

He ran along the rocky area, hearing Deguere follow. Caine made a zigzag pattern among the rocks to present a hard target, but he did not know what lay ahead and was afraid he was about to box himself in unwittingly.

Still, there was nothing to do but go on. The rocks became more rugged and sloped upward, and as he scrambled up, his grazed leg throbbed. He came across the crest of the rise, teetered for a moment, then fell into space.

He caught himself on jutting stones that felt like razors under his fingers. He was swinging over a rock pit about thirty feet deep. He looked down; in the cool shadows at its base he saw slithering, writhing motion. He heard a brief rattle. His fingers slipped a little on the stones.

Deguere was above him then, laughing. "Simon, my friend, you've done it now! And I do believe I see rattlers down there. Dark, cool places attract them, you know. It's a pity, because they will make it hard to get your corpse out. But I'll manage. Have to take some identifying portion to Montrose, you know.

"I almost hate to kill you, Caine. All these months of following you have made you something like an old friend to me. But all things must end, eh?"

Deguere thumbed back the hammer of his pistol and aimed. Caine fought the reflexive tendency to close his eyes; he would die looking Deguere in the face, unflinching.

From nowhere Keelan appeared directly behind Deguere. With a shout the boy pushed with his arms, shoving Deguere out. The detective screamed, sent winging into space the bullet intended for Caine, then fell writhing inches past Caine. He dropped into the pit. Caine and Keelan both heard the horrible crunch when he hit the rocks below, and then the rattling and movement of the rattlers that sank fangs into the fleshy form that had disturbed them.

Keelan, crying, reached down for Caine.

"It's no use, boy. I'd just pull you in," Caine said. "It's going to be up to me to get out."

Caine closed his eyes now, summoning his strength. Muscles contracting, he pulled up, inch by inch, then groped out with his right hand to find a better handhold. He did find one, then his left foot located a toehold on the rock. On it he pushed up, which enabled him to find a hold for his left hand. From there on he climbed carefully and slowly, sweat pouring off him in the sun and blood running down his hands from torn fingertips.

"You can do it, Mr. Simon," Keelan urged through his tears. "Just an inch or two more."

One final heave, and Caine was up. He rolled onto the

rocks beside Keelan and caught his breath. Keelan knelt and touched Caine's shoulder, patting and stroking it almost as if he were giving affection to a pup or a kitten.

"Are you really my uncle?" he asked.

"I sure am," Caine said, still panting for air.

Ria de Velasco was the first to see them returning. She was out emptying a washpot about sunset and looked up when she heard a whinny. Orion was well-bandaged and rode gingerly, hanging back somewhat behind Caine and Keelan. Ria lifted her hands toward the sky and let out a yelp of delight, then ran back into the house shouting for Rosalita and Brice.

Caine watched the doorway in nervous anticipation, hoping against hope that Brice would walk out on his own legs. The guilt of leaving his own brother crippled was a torment to Caine.

"Where's my pa, Uncle Simon?" Keelan asked.

"Probably inside, Keelan." He swallowed, dreading to tell the boy that his father might be unable to walk out to meet him. "Keelan, when I left, he was—"

Brice came to the doorway. On foot. His limp seemed worse, but he was walking. Caine's face brightened with a big grin.

"Pa!" Keelan yelled, dismounting and running toward him. "Pa!"

Brice walked clumsily out, knelt, and spread his arms. Keelan ran into them and wrapped his own arms around his father's neck. With smiles, kisses, and tears father and son were reunited.

Caine dismounted and helped Orion off his horse. They had waited two days after Keelan's rescue to begin the trip home, allowing Orion some time to start healing, though not nearly as much as he had really needed. Caine was grateful the bullets had passed cleanly through—otherwise they would have faced a much rougher prospect.

Rosalita came to Caine and Orion. Caine greeted her and realized just how much he had been thinking about the beautiful Mexican lady while he was away. She went to

Orion's other side and slipped her arm around his back; in so doing she touched Caine, and to him her touch seemed electric.

"You are badly hurt, Orion?" she asked.

"I'll make it. Just let me lie down."

They got him inside and into bed, then Caine and Rosalita went back outside. Caine paused at the door, where Ria already stood beaming, and Rosalita went to Brice and Keelan. She knelt and hugged the boy.

"They make a good family, no?" Ria said.

"Family?"

"*Sí,* Señor Caine. In the time you have been gone, many things have happened. Brice and Rosalita are to be married."

Caine looked the other way for a few moments. "I'm happy for them," he said at last.

That night, Orion told Caine that when he was healed up, he would become his partner. Ride with him from there on out.

No, Caine responded. Everywhere I go men try to kill me. I've got a name and a reputation and I'd just be a danger to you.

Orion said, that doesn't matter—I'm already wanted for killing and it'll be just the same for me. Besides, I'd be proud to ride with you.

So Caine smiled. I'd be proud, too, he said.

Brice and Rosalita talked about the wedding, about the family they would become, and about how they would start with little but somehow build a happy home. Brice told Keelan that he had heard only two days ago that his grandfather was gone, and now they would be on their own. The Kensington empire was no more, and there was no inheritance but debt and trouble. Keelan was saddened by the news about Garth, but a glow of happiness so permeated Ria de Velasco's *casa* that bad feelings just couldn't last here tonight. Soon he was smiling again.

Caine sat in the corner and watched it all. Brice came to him late in the evening.

"Simon, things aren't like they were before. From now

on we'll be together, brothers again. I don't know just what I'll be doing, but I'll have a good wife in Rosalita, and Keelan will have a good mother again. I'll make a place for Orion. And I want you to be with us, too."

"Thank you, Brice. I'm obliged for that."

"Good. We'll talk more about it in the morning, then."

"So we will."

It was hours later before they settled for sleep. In the darkness Caine rose and gathered his things. Keelan heard him and got up.

"Uncle Simon? What are you doing?"

"Hush, Keelan. I got to go."

"But Pa said—"

"I know. But it can never be that way. Do me a favor and don't wake them up, all right?"

"All right." Keelan watched Caine awhile longer. "Will you come back?"

"Maybe. If I can."

Caine put on his hat and went to the door. He stopped and looked around the *casa*, remembering again his own home and family, long gone from him.

"So long, Keelan. You take care of your pa and your mother. Be the man I know you are."

"I will."

Caine opened the door and stepped into the darkness.

"I love you, Uncle Simon," Keelan said as Caine walked away.

Caine did not turn. "I love you, too," he said. He kept walking until he reached the barn. He saddled his mount and rode away, and when he looked back, Keelan had closed the door.

CAINE'S TRAIL
is the fifth Bantam western by
CAMERON JUDD,
and if you enjoyed this book
you will enjoy his sixth novel for Bantam,

BAD NIGHT
AT
DRY CREEK

Here is an exciting preview of this new western novel, to be published in November, 1989. It will be available wherever Bantam titles are sold.

Turn the page for a sample of BAD NIGHT AT DRY CREEK by Cameron Judd.

Chapter 1

Charley Hanna shivered in the chilly Colorado wind but refused to return to the house. Instead he paced about the yard, smoking, casting occasional glances over his shoulder toward the door, watching wispy chimney smoke rising black against the gray sky. He would have liked to sit by the fire where it was warm, but the old lady had never liked him to smoke indoors, and with the doctor there and the threat of death hanging so heavy inside those walls, it was more comfortable outside, even with the cold. At least a man could smoke.

He looked once more at the house and wondered if the old lady was all right. He tossed his cigarette down into the dirty snow and listened to the faint sizzling sound it made as he dug into his vest pocket for his tobacco pouch.

"The old lady," he muttered to himself. What way was that for a man to think of his own mother?

But that was how his father had always referred to her, and there had been no lack of love on his part. And Charley loved her too, and worried about her now that she was ailing. If Pa were alive, he wouldn't have stood seeing her so sick. He had been a strong public servant all his days, but when it came to Ma he had been weak as mush. A lot of men were like that, Charley mused. Look unflinching down the muzzle of a rifle and then wilt away around women. That's the way Pa had been, and the way Charley was.

Everyone thought Charley was like his pa in almost

every way. After all, he had taken over the same job as town marshal here in Dry Creek. He walked with the same slump, wore the same pistol, and spoke with the same slow drawl.

It had been hard when Pa had passed on, but Charley had made it. At least Pa had died on his bed in a natural way, not choking out his life with a chest full of slugs like it might have been. Things were more civilized now than they had been in Pa's day.

Ma. How was she? What was taking that fool doctor so long? It was hard to believe she was sick; it had always seemed to Charley that she would live forever. But it had been two months now since she had even been out of bed, and every day she looked a bit weaker. And then last night something had happened—and now the doctor had been in there the longest time, and Charley half longed and half dreaded to see him come out.

Another cigarette fizzled out in the snow. Charley kicked up a piece of snow and frozen turf, then glanced once more toward the door. It opened and Charley's newest cigarette, not yet crimped shut, dropped from his fingers. Kathy Denning had come to the door.

"Kathy—is the doc..."

Dr. Eugene Hopkins came out of the door behind Kathy, pulling on his worn coat. He had worn that same coat as long as Charley had known him.

He didn't given Charley a chance to ask how Ma was doing.

"Charley, I've always been straight with all my patients and their families, and I won't change now. Your Ma is in a bad way, and I don't have high hopes for her."

"What's the matter with her?"

"Blood clot hit her brain. It's the same thing that killed your Pa."

Charley opened his mouth to speak, then realized suddenly there was really nothing to say. Dr. Hopkins coughed and sent out a white cloud of steam from his lips.

"Can you say how long she has, Doctor?" Kathy asked in a choked voice.

The old man grunted. "Only the Lord can say, girl. That's beyond anything an old country doctor can predict."

Charley thanked the doctor and moved up on the porch beside Kathy. The old medic wheezed out to his buggy, coughing loudly, his shoulders stooped. It took him a long time and a lot of effort to crawl up into the driver's seat. He clicked his tongue and jerked the lines, and the buggy clattered off on the frozen rock road.

"His cough is bad. I wouldn't be surprised if it was consumption," Kathy said.

Charley said nothing, but turned and entered the house. Kathy looked after him thoughtfully.

Sarah Redding pulled her shawl closer around her and stared out the window. The sky was gray, cold, and threatening. So far the snows had been meager, but it wouldn't be long until the first heavy snow blanketed the Rockies and the Dry Creek community. Sarah was grateful for the warmth of the cabin and the stock of firewood outside. She had prepared well for winter, carefully re-chinking the cracks in the wall, laying in supplies for months ahead. When the big snows came she would be ready.

She looked around the cabin. It was lonesome, but she tried to ignore the feeling. She had learned to shove it aside, to lose it in the bustle of everyday business. It helped her to forget the emptiness since John died.

John... what a husband he had been, working hard, building a secure home for them, talking in anticipation of the family they would raise together. When he had died, crushed beneath a tree that was to provide winter fuel, she had almost given up hope. But there was no choice but to do the best she could. She hoped many times on her bed at night that John was proud of her.

The homestead seemed empty now without a man's hand at work on it. But she had a fierce pride in all she had accomplished, and was determined she would make it.

Her attention was drawn suddenly to something down the road—a movement where it curved around the trees. A rider was slowly approaching, his horse's breath sending out double puffs of white mist. She felt apprehensive. There were few riders out this way; who could it be?

Her heart leaped suddenly. Maybe it was Charley Hanna! It looked like his horse. Her breath quickened and a smile played on her lips. Charley was the only man since John had died who excited her. Her hands fumbled at the knot of her apron, and she wondered where she had left her comb.

She glanced again out the window, and her heart fell. It wasn't Charley, but a stranger. She eyed him with suspicion. Into the yard he rode, but did not dismount.

She peeped around the curtain and frowned, then stepped back into the center of the cabin, unnerved. The stranger didn't call, nor dismount; instead he stared silently at the cabin. Nervously she reached above the cabinet against the wall and removed a small pistol. She checked it. It was loaded. Her hand felt cold against the bone handle.

He called out then, softly. Strange... something in his voice was not right. She looked out the window again. He was pale and trembling, and apparently not only from the cold.

She saw him slump over the saddlehorn, then slide limply to the earth. One foot still hung in the stirrup; his horse stepped restlessly. She saw a stain of red on his side.

Sarah threw open the door. The cold air struck her, chilling her through the thin fabric of her dress. She ran to the man's side, hesitated uncertainly, then loosened his boot heel from the stirrup. His leg fell deadweight to the dirt, and he groaned.

"Mister?"

He moaned again. Feeling she had to do something, anything, Sarah rolled him over on his back and looked into his face.

A rough growth of beard darkened his jaws, but he looked pallid and ill. Sarah realized suddenly that this man had been shot.

"Mister... can you hear me?"

His eyes opened, lined with pain, bloodshot. "I'm shot, lady."

"What can I do?" For some unaccountable reason Sarah felt she might cry.

"Help me inside—got to have water, rest..."

"You'll have to stand. There's no way I can carry you."

He moaned and shut his eyes. "I can stand, if you'll help me."

Trembling with fear and cold, Sarah reached down and grasped his hand. He strained upward, groaning as he sat up, then weakly he struggled to his feet. Growing even paler, he leaned against his saddle for support.

"Can you make it?" Sarah asked.

"Yeah... just help me."

"Lean against my shoulder—careful."

Her fear forgotten now, covered over by concern for this man's welfare, she put her arm around his waist, supporting him as best she could, and led him toward the house. With several groans and winces of pain he struggled up onto the porch and through the door.

"This way, mister. You can lie down."

He leaned against her as they moved toward the bed in the corner. She tried to ease him down gently, but he went suddenly limp and collapsed. She lifted his legs onto the soft straw tick, then worked at removing his boots.

He breathed a little easier as he relaxed on the tick, but seemed to be fluctuating between consciousness and a swoon. She eyed his bloody shirt. It would have to come off, and the wound would surely need cleaning.

She picked up a pair of scissors and began snipping away at the clotted fabric. The man stirred and came back to consciousness.

"Much obliged, ma'am."

"What's your name?"

"Murphy. Willy Murphy." His voice was very strained.

Murphy. A familiar name, but she could attach no particular significance to it. "How did this happen to you?"

He smiled sardonically. "Let's just say I had a family disagreement."

She frowned. He was being cagey for a man who easily might be dead if not for her. She realized that this fellow could be on the wrong side of the law. She stopped snipping at the shirt.

"You better be straight with me. I don't have to keep you here, you know." She was surprised at her own boldness.

He smiled his strange little smile once more and nodded.

"I guess you're right. But I have to have your promise that..." He chuckled painfully. "It doesn't matter. I've had it anyway."

His words confused her, but she sensed that he was about to tell her something she wasn't sure she wanted to hear.

"Lady, I can't expect you to make no promise, but I'd be obliged if you didn't go to the law with what I tell you." He paused and looked at her expectantly. She said nothing, and he gave a little philosophical grunt and went on.

"The law's after me. I was in on a bank robbery in Denver a few weeks back."

Her nostrils flared. "Was it the law who did this to you?"

He laughed weakly at that. "No, lady. My brother did it. Can you believe it, my own brother!" He laughed again, even though it clearly hurt him.

"Why?"

"I took the money for myself. Never did learn to share when I was a little feller."

"Where is the money?" Sarah felt sudden embarrassment when he gave her a probing look. "I didn't mean...I don't want it for myself...oh, blast you. I don't owe you any explanations!"

"No ma'am, you don't. You might have heard of my brother, Noah Murphy."

Her eyes widened. "You're one of the Murphy gang!"

He saw the fear in her. "Easy, lady...I ain't going to hurt you. I don't even have my gun anymore. Besides, I got nothing against you. I won't even blame you if you go to the law, though I hope you don't. It was Noah that shot me. Y'see, I took that cash from the Denver robbery and hid it good, where nobody could find it. Noah didn't like that, and proved it with this bullet. I barely got away from him. Thought I would die before I found someplace to rest. If it wasn't for you and your place here I might be out there freezing to death right now."

"Glad I could help." The words were very uncertain.

"I ain't going to stay here long, lady. I'll be on my way long before Noah gets on my trail. I just need a little rest, and some food, if you can spare it."

"You need a doctor."

"'Fraid not, ma'am. Y'see, doctors ask questions, then they go to the law. I can't afford that—you understand?"

"I understand you'll die if you don't get that slug out of you."

"You just leave me to rest, ma'am. I'll be out of your way before sundown tomorrow."

"Dr. Hopkins is a good man—you can trust him."

"No." His tone frightened her this time.

She drew away. "All right, then. But if you die you can't blame nobody but yourself."

He lay back. "Oh, I don't know—seems to me that ol' Noah had a little something to do with it." Within moments he was asleep.

Sarah cooked some broth and made hot coffee. When she awoke Willie Murphy about an hour later he was hot with fever, and could take only a little broth. The coffee he finished, then lay back once more into slumber.

It was dark outside, and the wind was howling. Sarah kept a fire burning. She sat at her window and stared out into the darkness, listening to Willy Murphy's fevered talk in his sleep.

Fine flakes of snow swirled about, coming to rest on the frozen earth, settling on the woodpile. It might be sooner than she had expected that the first real blizzard came. When that happened travel would be difficult. She might be stranded here in this house, alone with this wounded man, waiting for the sound of horses outside that would signal the arrival of Noah Murphy.

The sun had hardly risen the following morning when Sarah was on the road to Dry Creek. The decision had been made sometime after midnight. Willy Murphy was a criminal, a self-confessed bank robber, and she had no obligation to do anything other than provide him shelter until the law could take him to where he belonged. And in Dry Creek that law was Charley Hanna. She would see him, tell him what had happened, and in the company of Dr. Hopkins, he could come with her back to the cabin. She would get this outlaw out of her life before anything happened—particularly before Noah Murphy arrived.

The cold town of Dry Creek was stirring to life as she drove her wagon into the street. Smoke rose from every chimney, and she smelled the aroma of sizzling bacon and boiling coffee. Her stomach was empty, but she ignored the rumblings of it and made her way to the jailhouse.

What would Charley think, seeing her coming in so early? She wondered if he realized how he made her heart race whenever she saw him striding down the street, tall and powerful. She was sure he had no corresponding thoughts about her. Charley seemed to be a man with little time for women, and little interest in them. If he had a woman at all it was Katherine Denning, who cared for Charley's ailing mother. There had been occasions when Sarah had seen Katherine looking at Charley in a way that clearly showed how she admired him. It didn't seem that Charley had noticed those looks, but one day he surely would and then he would be gone as far as Sarah was concerned.

She couldn't suppress a shiver of anticipation as she stepped onto the jailhouse porch and knocked on the door. When she heard the latch opening she smiled.

Her face fell when Bo Myers opened the door. The young deputy grinned at her through a scruffy beard. His teeth were yellow and had prominent gaps between them. A true man of the earth, this Bo Myers, and he smelled and looked the part. Sarah wondered how Charley could put up with him.

"Hello, Bo. Is Charley in?"

"Yep. Come on in, Miss Redding. Charley's over here eating breakfast."

Sarah stepped inside and Bo shut out the cold wind. Sarah smiled at Charley, who was rising from his chair behind the desk and wiping a trace of gravy from his mustache. She noticed that he looked weary and rather sad.

Sarah smiled at Charley, feeling a bit awkward. Bo kept flashing his yellow, snaggle-toothed grin.

"Hello, Sarah," Charley said. "Didn't expect to see you this morning."

"That breakfast smells good."

Charley fairly jumped toward the pot-bellied stove. "Well, here—have some bacon and coffee. Bo, fry up an egg or two for Sarah."

"That won't be necessary, thank you." She recalled Charley's mother was sick, and asked about her.

"Ma ain't doing too good, Sarah. Dr. Hopkins don't expect her to live long. I'm worried about her."

"I'm so sorry. Mrs. Hanna has always meant a lot to everybody in Dry Creek. She'll get better—you'll see."

Charley smiled and Sarah felt warmth steal over her.

"Something wrong out your way, Sarah?"

"I've got some trouble, Charley. I hope you can help." Charley looked at her blankly, then with increasing concern as she outlined what had occurred. When she mentioned Noah Murphy, he exhaled sharply and frowned.

"I heard the Murphy brothers had been involved in that Denver bank robbery, but I had no idea they had come up this way. You say it was Noah who shot Willy?"

"That's what he said."

"How bad hurt is he?"

"It looks bad. That's why I want to get Dr. Hopkins to go along with us. I brought the wagon into town. I figure maybe we can ride Murphy back on that."

"Yeah—good idea. It's a good thing you came, Sarah. Men like Willy Murphy belong in a cell."

Charley rose from his chair and strapped on his gunbelt. He cut a handsome figure, and with his gun at his hip, he appeared deadly and powerful. It was good to know that Dry Creek was under his protection. Sarah recalled seeing Charley's father when she was a girl; Charley was the very image of him. As she looked at Charley Sarah's fears of the Murphy brothers diminished. With Charley Hanna along she would be safe.

"Bo, you stay here and look out for things while I'm gone." Charley put on his hat.

"Dang, boss, nothing will happen around here. It never does. You might need help with Murphy. Let me go with you."

"No, Bo. There won't be trouble from nobody as hurt as Willy Murphy. We'll be back in no time."

Charley pulled on a heavy leather, coat, lined with fur that spilled out around the neck, and on his head he placed the battered, weathered old hat that had become so identified with him that most people saw it as an extension of him. He put his hand on Sarah's shoulder and escorted her out the door. She felt a thrill of warmth.

They found Dr. Hopkins sipping a cup of coffee beside a roaring fire in his office. He welcomed them in cordially, doing his best to silence the coughs that wracked his body at intervals.

"Coffee?" he offered.

"No thanks. We've got business."

"A man's been shot," Sarah explained.

Dr. Hopkins' eyes grew wide. "Hunting accident?"

"No. And it ain't just any man, either. It's Willy Murphy," Charley said.

Dr. Hopkins looked blankly at Charley. "Who?"

"Willy Murphy. One of the Murphy brothers—Noah's brother."

The doctor nodded understandingly. "Where?"

Sarah once again ran through her story. She had hardly

finished before the physician was up, gathering items into his medical bag, then reaching for his hat and coat on the wall pegs.

"I'll patch him up good enough so you can put him behind bars, Charley. If he's still alive."

Charley started to head for the stable to get his horse, then thought better of it. "I'll ride with you, Sarah." They went outside together.

Sarah welcomed the prospect of riding all the way back to the cabin next to Charley. He climbed onto the driver's seat and took the reins in his big, rugged hands. Sarah climbed up beside him, and Dr. Hopkins followed. Sarah took advantage of the fact that Dr. Hopkins' wide rump required a lot of room on the seat, and she sat as closely as possible to Charley. He pretended not to notice, but she suspected he did.

The wagon clattered down the street and out of town. At the other end of the street Kathy Denning stared coldly through a curtained window, watching unhappily as Sarah Redding sat snugly beside Charley. She released the curtain and turned back into the chilly room.

Charley whistled as he drove the team, but Sarah could tell he was tense. About a half-mile out of town he began talking about the Murphy boys.

"Those two are a rough pair," he said. "Twin boys, both mean as snakes since they was little. Take after their daddy. Pa talked about old Jack Murphy a lot—Lead Jack, they called him. Laid claim to a quick gun and an ornery disposition. Pa never met him—said if he had it might have come to a shootout, Pa being a man of the law and all. Pa admitted Lead Jack was one gunfighter he wasn't sure he could beat. Lead Jack wound up on the end of a rope. That's exactly where Willy and Noah belong, too—Noah more than Willy, from what I hear. It's a shame there had to be two of them boys—double trouble, y'know."

"Do you think Willy will be a problem?" asked Dr. Hopkins.

"I doubt it. He's wounded, and Sarah said he didn't have a gun. To be honest, I think we might find him dead."

"It's likely. A wound like Sarah described can drain the life from a man. I've seen plenty in my day."

Both Sarah and Charley knew that Hopkins truly had. He had led a rough-and-tumble life amid the wildest mining towns and cattle camps throughout the region, patching up wounds, taking his pay in whiskey and chickens as often as in cash, and moving on from town to town like a drifter. It was only when age started putting rust on his joints that he finally settled down in Dry Creek. He had become a close friend of the Hanna family and almost everyone else in town.

The talk continued for the duration of the trip until they reached the bend of the road. Charley pulled the wagon to a stop barely out of sight of the house. Sarah looked at him expectantly.

"I'll go on in from here alone," he said. "If you hear me holler bring the wagon on in," he said. Sarah nodded.

"I'll go in with you," Dr. Hopkins said.

"No. There wouldn't be much you could do without a gun. And I would rather have you here with Sarah."

Charley climbed down from the wagon seat and hitched up his trousers before striding firmly toward the house. Sarah noted that he loosened his pistol in its holster.

The house was silent as Charley approached. No smoke came from the chimney. The place looked deserted. Charley nonetheless felt a keen sense of apprehension, and he continued with great caution. His boots made a crackling sound as they trod on the freezing snow coating the ground. Fresh snow was lightly falling, and the wind whistled around the eaves of the cabin.

Charley looked at the windows. Still no sign of life inside—no movement of the curtains nor hint of a passing body in the darkness of the cabin interior. He reached the door. The cabin was as silent as death. Carefully he reached out to the latch and turned it gently.

The door opened onto a dark room. The last coals of the

fireplace cast a faint red glow across the floor. Still no sound.

Charley stepped inside, drawing his pistol at the same time. He looked around the interior of the cabin, searching for Willy Murphy.

A NOTE FROM THE AUTHOR

I was born in 1956 in Cookeville, Tennessee, and I remain a resident Tennessean. I wrote my first western at age twenty-two; and now I am writing exclusively for Bantam.

My interest in the American West is just part of a broader interest in the frontier. I am fascinated by the vast westward expanses on the other side of the Mississippi, but I am equally intrigued by the original American West: the area west of the Appalachians and east of the Mississippi. I hope someday to write fiction set in that older frontier at the time of its settlement, in addition to traditional westerns.

My interest in westerns was sparked in early childhood by television, movies, and books. I appreciate both the fact of the West and the myth of the West; and believe both aspects have a valid place in popular fiction.

I received an undergraduate degree in English and journalism, plus teaching accreditation in English and history, from Tennessee Technological University in 1979. Since that time I have been a newspaperman by profession, both as a writer and editor. Today I am on the editorial staff of the daily newspaper in Greeneville, Tennessee, one of the state's most historic towns.

Greeneville is the seat of the county that contributed one of America's original frontier heroes to the world—Davy Crockett. Greeneville was also the hometown of President Andrew Johnson and was for several years the capital of the Lost State of Franklin—an eighteenth-century political experiment that came close to achieving statehood.

I live in rural Greene County with my wife, Rhonda, and children, Matthew, Laura, and Bonnie.

Cameron Judd